"I couldn't have gotten through this without you, Stephanie."

"Oh, you would have managed all right."

"I don't think so. You're the first person I thought of to help out down here. I can see now my instinct was right."

He lifted his hand slowly and touched her hair. "You have such beautiful hair. I've never seen it down like this." His words were quiet, practically a whisper.

"It gets in the way."

He laughed lightly at her answer. "I'd imagine that the problem is more like *men* get in the way," he replied. "This one can't resist...."

Her impossibly handsome boss was about to kiss her.

And she was going to let him.

Was this really happening to her?

Dear Reader,

No matter what the weather is like, I always feel like March 1st is the beginning of spring. So let's celebrate that just-around-the-corner thaw with, for starters, another of Christine Rimmer's beloved BRAVO FAMILY TIES books. In *The Bravo Family Way,* a secretive Las Vegas mogul decides he "wants" a beautiful preschool owner who's long left the glittering lights and late nights of Vegas behind. But she hadn't counted on the charms of Fletcher Bravo. No woman could resist him for long....

Victoria Pade's *The Baby Deal,* next up in our FAMILY BUSINESS continuity, features wayward son Jack Hanson finally agreeing to take a meeting with a client—only perhaps he got a little too friendly too fast? She's pregnant, and he's...well, he's not sure what he is, quite frankly. In Judy Duarte's *Call Me Cowboy,* a New York City girl is in desperate need of a detective with a working knowledge of Texas to locate the mother she's never known. Will she find everything she's looking for, courtesy of T. J. "Cowboy" Whittaker? In *She's the One,* Patricia Kay's conclusion to her CALLIE'S CORNER CAFÉ series, a woman who's always put her troublesome younger sister's needs before her own finds herself torn by her attraction to the handsome cop who's about to place said sister under arrest. Lois Faye Dyer's new miniseries, THE McCLOUDS OF MONTANA, which features two feuding families, opens with *Luke's Proposal.* In it, the daughter of one family is forced to work together with the son of the other— with very unexpected results! And in *A Bachelor at the Wedding* by Kate Little, a sophisticated Manhattan tycoon finds himself relying more and more on his Brooklyn-bred assistant (yeah, Brooklyn)— and not just for business.

So enjoy, and come back next month—the undisputed start of spring....

Gail

Please address questions and book requests to:
Silhouette Reader Service
U.S.: 3010 Walden Ave., P.O. Box 1325, Buffalo, NY 14269
Canadian: P.O. Box 609, Fort Erie, Ont. L2A 5X3

A BACHELOR AT THE WEDDING

KATE LITTLE

Silhouette

SPECIAL EDITION

Published by Silhouette Books

America's Publisher of Contemporary Romance

SILHOUETTE BOOKS

ISBN 0-373-24746-X

A BACHELOR AT THE WEDDING

Copyright © 2006 by Anne Canadeo

This edition published by arrangement with Harlequin Books S.A.

® and TM are trademarks of Harlequin Books S.A., used under license.
Trademarks indicated with ® are registered in the United States Patent
and Trademark Office, the Canadian Trade Marks Office and in other
countries.

Visit Silhouette Books at www.eHarlequin.com

Printed in U.S.A.

Books by Kate Little

Silhouette Special Edition
A Bachelor at the Wedding #1746

Silhouette Desire

Jingle Bell Baby #1043
Husband for Keeps #1276
The Determined Groom #1302
The Millionaire Takes a Bride #1349
The Bachelorette #1401
Tall, Dark & Cranky #1422
Plain Jane & Doctor Dad #1436

KATE LITTLE

claims to have lots of experience with romance—"the *fictional* kind, that is," she is quick to clarify. She has been both an author and an editor of romance fiction for over fifteen years. She believes that a good romance will make the reader experience all the tension, thrills and agony of falling madly, deeply and wildly in love. She enjoys watching the characters in her books go crazy for each other, but hates to see the blissful couple disappear when it's time for them to live happily ever after. In addition to writing romance novels, Kate also writes fiction and nonfiction for young adults. She lives on Long Island with her husband and daughter.

Chapter One

She was so lovely. Beautiful, really.

He hadn't realized it at first. But now the thought ran through his head every time he looked at her. Some men might not notice her. Some might even find her plain. But some men didn't have his taste and experience when it came to women.

She wasn't the flashy type. Not this one, Matt Harding mused. Stephanie Rossi possessed a more subtle, richer kind of beauty. Genuine and unadorned. One that worked on a man. Got under his skin. Into his blood.

He ought to know. If half of what the gossip columnists in this town reported was true, he was one of the city's richest and most eligible bachelors, and changed beautiful partners as easily as he changed his custom-made suits. While the legend was exaggerated—as legends often are—Matt knew the womanizer image was well earned.

Stephanie Rossi had worked with him nearly a month now. He fully expected that, by now, he'd be accustomed to her looks, and immune to her appeal. But in fact, as the days passed, the affliction had only grown worse. Especially when she flashed that brilliant, heart-stopping smile. A smile that penetrated deep into his soul.

He hated when she was nice to him or seemed on the verge of letting down her guard. That made it so much harder. Sometimes he found himself purposely gruff to keep her at arm's length. Or maybe growling was just a way of venting pent-up frustrations.

Three weeks on the job and she must think I'm an ogre, a horror. A total…jackass. No help for it. Let her think what she will. He knew he had no choice but to play the role of the tough, impossible-to-please boss.

Luckily, she didn't smile or relax around him all that much. She certainly hadn't tried to take advantage of her very advantageous opportunity, working side by side with the hotel chain's owner. He knew some women would try to exploit the opportunity. Offering more than their professional talents. But not Stephanie Rossi. He'd wager that she didn't have a conniving bone in her body. The very shapely, tempting body that it was.

She was all business. Professional and impersonal—or at least, trying to make that impression.

Efficient and sharp, but also graced with rare skills for soothing a disgruntled employee or a dissatisfied guest. An invaluable talent in any business setting, but especially a hotel.

When her name was first put forward as the temporary replacement for his personal assistant, Matt had
balked. It was sexist of him, but he preferred a male assistant, one he could bellow at when the mood struck
without having to manage a tearful outburst, or some
other variety of female hysteria. Besides, he knew
Stephanie Rossi had only been in her job at the Harding
Plaza as an assistant manager in the operations department for barely a month. Even if she was the Wonder
Girl her boss claimed, Matt didn't see how she could
come to the executive suite after such a short time. But
finally—very doubtful it would work out—he'd agreed
to try her for a week.

From day one, she'd been cool and competent—and
for a girl born and bred in Brooklyn—a class act all the
way. He tested her, even unfairly. But she'd handled the
challenges admirably. She was certainly not the chat-
tering, flailing female he'd expected. Far from it. She
was so quiet, sometimes he hardly knew she was there.
Well, he was always subtly aware of her presence—like
a low-frequency vibration—even when she was off in
her own office, a thick wall between them.

He'd been thinking about promoting her perma-
nently to the head office. With her brains and manage-
ment skills, she'd be a great asset to him. He had no
doubt.

Just as often he had the impulse to send her packing,
back to her regular job in operations. He knew by now
that his attraction to her wasn't wearing off as he'd
expected. Quite the opposite. It was growing by the
hour, building up speed and momentum. Like a boulder
bouncing down a mountainside. Threatening to start an
avalanche any minute now.

His regular assistant, Jerry Fields, was out on a medical leave and might not return to work for at least three months. Matt didn't think he could last, working side by side with Stephanie all that time. After only a week, he was about to blow some crucial male fuse. Every time she gave him that small, inscrutable Mona Lisa smile, he had half a mind to jump her bones.

Impossible, of course. For one thing, he had an ironclad rule about romancing employees. He simply didn't do it.

Stephanie Rossi was not the first to challenge his vow. Though no woman so far had ever tested his will-power as intensely. And she wasn't even trying. But Matt was determined. He wouldn't break down and give in. Not even for this girl, this very rare find. This dark-haired jewel.

Still, he couldn't help watching her while she sat nearby, completely focused on her work, unaware of his secret scrutiny. Seated in an armchair across from his desk, her lovely features set in an expression of deep concentration, she reviewed a weekly summary of the hotel's activity. He had a copy of the same report and should have been studying it, too. But his thoughts kept straying, his gaze kept wandering, feasting on the mere sight of her, though he could never get his fill.

He loved the color of her hair. In the late afternoon light that streamed through the large windows behind his desk, her smooth, dark mane was a rich shade of coffee, shimmering with red lights. So far, he'd only seen her wear it in this simple, conservative style, pulled back from her face and twisted in a loose knot just above her nape. A prim, professional look that suited her manner.

He imagined how it would look undone, falling down her back and across her shoulders in a silky cascade. How far would it reach? It looked quite long, rolled up in that complicated twist. It would certainly fall below her shoulders. Her bare shoulders, Matt decided. Her skin was flawless, smooth and fair, and the small pearl earrings she wore perfectly matched the radiant quality of her complexion.

His gaze slowly followed her profile, her high cheekbones, long, straight nose and wide, sensual mouth. Her thick lashes now shadowed her large dark eyes. Eyes that reflected warmth, intelligence and a touching innocence that Matt thought amazing to find in this city. A quality that unraveled him at times.

If it was true that eyes were the windows of the soul, then Stephanie Rossi possessed a beautiful spirit. Not that she was without a sense of humor. At times, she'd surprised him with her witty comebacks, sharp one-liners that effectively put *him* in line. Normally, he didn't take any back talk from subordinates. But he did from her, her comments turning his moods into something more…reasonable.

She suddenly looked up at him, curiosity reflected in her shimmering gaze. A faint blush rose in her cheeks. She'd caught him looking at her and she felt self-conscious. He felt self-conscious, too. An unfamiliar reaction. He forced himself to maintain a blank expression.

"Looks like there's been a small downturn in occupancy this week," she said.

"Yes, I noticed." He flipped a page on the report, not really aware of what he was reading.

She glanced at some notes she'd made in the margin

of the page. "Gross receipts in room revenue and food service will be off about eight percent this week. But we should make up the difference quickly. There are two weddings booked for the weekend, big society affairs. We'll have some overflow guests, I'm sure. And the International Association of Journalists is winding up their convention tonight with a banquet in the main ballroom. We've already scheduled extra staff at the front desk to get the conference attendees checked out quickly tomorrow."

Matt nodded, his expression revealing neither approval nor disapproval. Secretly, he marveled at her ability to evaluate this thick package in moments. She also had a fantastic memory for detail. She knew what was happening on-site at any given moment and could anticipate the most improbable glitch. He already trusted her to watch over the daily events, freeing him to attend to larger issues.

Once again, Stephanie had it covered. Their meeting should be over. Yet, he couldn't quite manage to excuse her. Once he did, she'd be gone. Out of his sight for two entire days. How would he distract himself for the entire weekend, waiting to see her again?

Oh, yes, he had a date. Scheduled to start later this evening, it would probably melt over into Saturday night as well, moving from the city to his house in East Hampton. Matt felt a muscle in his jaw tighten as he pretended to review the report once more. He tried to picture the woman he was presently dating—a stunning entertainment reporter, Jenna Malone. But he couldn't quite keep the sexy blonde's face in his mind's eye....

He noticed Stephanie discreetly check her watch. It was almost six. Late to be kept working on a Friday night. Maybe she had a date, too? The thought of her rushing off to meet some boyfriend—some undeserving, immature punk, he was sure—irritated him. Though he knew he had no right whatsoever.

"Who'll be on-site tonight for the conference banquet? Tom Daley?" he asked brusquely, naming the head of the banquet department.

"No, I don't think Tom's around tonight. His younger boy, Scott, is in a school play."

Leave it to Stephanie to learn such a small, personal detail. He'd known Daley for five years and could hardly recall that the man had children. She not only knew the kid's name, but probably knew the name of play and Scott's role in it.

Matt ran his hand carelessly through his thick, dark hair. He rose abruptly from his chair and walked around to the front of his desk, where Stephanie sat. He sensed her watching him, waiting to see what he would do next. He sensed her tension. Yet she sat totally composed. She wasn't afraid of him, he realized. She already knew his bark was worse than his bite. Especially where she was concerned.

"Well, someone ought to hang around tonight. Reporters are notorious gossips. We don't want them bad-mouthing Harding Hotels from here to Timbuktu."

"Good point. I'll find someone from Food and Beverage to stand by." She glanced at her watch again. "It's late. I'd better get to work on that. Anything else?"

She suddenly rose from her seat and looked up at him. She was standing quite close. Too close for comfort.

He felt an almost overwhelming urge to reach up and touch her cheek, to pull her into his arms. He breathed in the scent she wore, light but spicy and intriguing, an essence that drew him even closer. She stared directly at him; her warm dark gaze made him forget what he was about to say.

He quickly moved away and rubbed the back of his neck with his hand.

"You should have thought of this banquet issue before, Stephanie. Now you face the problem of finding someone to cover at the last minute."

She stood in the center of the room, standing very straight with her chin raised at an elegant, courageous tilt. She could take the heat; he'd grant her that. It wasn't really her fault. It was Tom Daley's. But of course, Stephanie didn't shift the blame. She wasn't the type.

"No problem. If I can't find anyone from the banquet department, I'll do it myself," she said simply.

He pursed his lips. That wasn't what he'd wanted at all, having her work late on a Friday night, cramping her social life...or was it? God, this woman was driving him crazy. And unlike so many others, she wasn't even *trying*.

"It's Friday night. I'm sure you have plans."

He hadn't meant to turn the conversation in a personal direction. The question had just slipped out. Her eyes widened in surprise.

"Yes, I do have plans," she admitted, slowly, "but I suppose I can...rearrange them in order to stay a bit longer."

Meet her boyfriend later, she meant. That image was even more vexing. He moved behind his desk and sat down hard in his chair. "Let's hope it doesn't come to that."

"I don't mind, really."

Her gaze met his again and he felt his temperature rise. She felt it, too. He was sure of it. He could tell by the way she suddenly looked away and stared down at the carpeting, a faint flush rising on her cheeks. She had the face of a Renaissance beauty, a perfect image from a fifteenth-century masterpiece.

He swallowed hard. He had to get her out of his office. Immediately.

The beep of the intercom interrupted his thoughts. He pressed a button and curtly addressed his secretary. "Yes, what is it?"

"A call for Ms. Rossi, on line three. They said it's an emergency."

"For me?" Stephanie's composed expression turned to alarm. "I can take it in my office."

"No, go ahead—" he insisted. He handed over the phone receiver and pressed the blinking button on the console.

"Hello?" Stephanie greeted the caller. Her expression at first looked quite concerned, then within moments, relaxed and almost amused.

"Yes, Nana," he heard her say. "No, it's all right. He isn't mad…." She glanced up at him, a small smile playing about her lips, as if they shared a private joke. He smiled back, feeling warm all over.

Stephanie finished the conversation quickly and handed back the phone. "Sorry about that."

"Is everything okay?"

"Nothing serious." He could see that she was trying hard not to smile, but finally she couldn't help herself. "You don't know my family. Their idea of an emergency is running out of sun-dried tomatoes. Or maybe if one of my sisters can't make it out to Brooklyn for Sunday dinner."

Matt laughed. He couldn't help himself. "You have dinner together every Sunday?"

"More or less. You could set your watch by the antipasto platter. It hits the table at one forty-five, precisely. Right after my parents get back from twelve o'clock mass."

She was making fun of her family, but she didn't know what it was to grow up without any feelings of warmth and belonging. His fondest memories of mealtimes were sharing dinner with the servants, down in the kitchen.

"It sounds…very nice. Very traditional."

Stephanie sighed and smiled again. "I guess. They're not really that bad. Medical excuses are accepted. If you have a signed note from a doctor."

He laughed again and Stephanie joined him. "Was that your grandmother?"

She nodded. "She couldn't reach my cell. My grandmother's card game was canceled so I don't have to run out to Brooklyn tonight to babysit for my sister. Nana's going to take over. So I guess I can stay and oversee the banquet."

Babysitting for her sister. Those were her Friday night plans. She was a nice woman…too nice for him.

"Your grandmother plays cards?"

Stephanie nodded. "Poker. Five card stud, with her 'posse' from the neighborhood. Every Friday night…unless there's something hot going on at St. Anthony's with the Golden Age Club. She just plays for pennies. She says games of chance keep your brain cells active."

Matt smiled and caught Stephanie's eye. "She sounds like quite a character."

"Definitely," Stephanie added with a rueful grin. "Maybe it's something in the water out there. They're all pretty nutty if you ask me."

She tucked the report under her arm, looking ready to conclude the conversation, but he was curious to know more.

"So your family lives in Brooklyn?"

"My parents, grandmother and all four sisters, including the three who are married."

"You have *four* sisters?" He smiled at the thought of four more versions of Stephanie. "Your poor father. Imagine paying for all those weddings. He must try to bribe you all to elope."

"I understand he makes an offer that's *almost* too good to refuse," she quipped. "But so far, all my sisters have gone the traditional route. He gets a break from his cousin who owns a catering hall. My youngest sister, Angie, is getting married a few weeks from now."

"A spring wedding. That is traditional." Matt eyed Stephanie. He imagined her going the same route, dressed in a long gown and trailing veil. Cream-colored satin would suit her perfectly. She'd be a vision—no doubt about it.

"That's four down, one to go," he tallied aloud.

"I'm not in any hurry." She shrugged. Something in her offhand tone made him think he may have offended her.

"I didn't mean to imply that you should be," he said.

"If only my family shared your opinion," she confided. "My life would be a lot easier."

"Really? Do they bother you much about it?"

"Only whenever I speak to them, or see them…or have contact of any form."

He laughed again, but he could see it bothered her. "That's not a very modern attitude. What about your career? They should be proud of you. You're excellent at your job and have a great future. You've come a long way for someone your age. I really mean it."

His praise pleased her. He liked bringing that bright smile to her face. It was the only compliment he'd given her all week, though he knew she deserved to hear much more.

"Thank you, Matt. That's kind of you to say. But no one has ever accused Dominic and Francesca Rossi of harboring a *modern* attitude."

Matt smiled in reply. He fiddled with a silver pen on his desktop. He should just let the conversation go and say good-night. But he was too curious to know more about her. For instance…was her romance with the accountant serious?

"What about your boyfriend? How does he feel about it?" he asked quietly.

Stephanie looked surprised again and he suddenly realized he'd given himself away, at least his knowledge about her private life. He'd asked around about her. He couldn't help it.

"I'm not seeing anyone special right now."

He pulled his gaze from hers and stared out the window. "Oh, you're not? I thought you had mentioned something about a boyfriend at some point?" he said vaguely.

"I don't think so. I just broke up with someone. It was a long relationship. We knew each other from grade school. But I don't think I ever mentioned it…."

Her voice trailed off on a puzzled note.

He cleared his throat. "Maybe not…I guess I confused you with someone else." He sat up in his high-backed leather chair. "Well, these things happen. Usually, it's all for the best."

"Yes, I'm sure of it." Her tone was very definite, he noticed, and she didn't look the least bit unhappy. Looked like she was the one who had ended the relationship. Even better, from his perspective.

So, the accountant was out of the picture. He felt a happy jolt and struggled to hide it. Okay, so she's not in a relationship. She's still off limits, pal. Just remember that.

Yet, when Matt looked up again, it was as if a huge flashing sign had popped up over her head: AVAILABLE!!! AVAILABLE!!

"Is there anything else?" Stephanie asked, completely back to business.

"I think that covers it," he replied quickly. "See you Monday."

He waved at her in a dismissing motion, suddenly knowing he had to get her out of his office, out of his sight. Or something would happen. Something momentarily wonderful, he was sure…but definitely regrettable in the long run.

She said good-night, then turned and walked to the door. He loved the way she moved. She was so graceful and elegant, her slim figure almost entirely camouflaged today in a sleek blue suit, a slit in the back of the straight skirt revealing a length of long, slim legs.

He heard the sound of the heavy door closing behind her and was suddenly alone in his office. He released a long harsh breath. One he had not even noticed he'd been holding.

This...*thing* he had about Stephanie Rossi was insane. If he didn't watch out, he'd end up embarrassing himself...embarrassing both of them. And maybe with a lawsuit on his hands for harassment as well, he reminded himself.

He ran his hand through his hair, picking up the subtle trace of Stephanie's perfume that still hung in the air.

He shook his head. "Harding, get a grip!"

Stephanie escaped Matthew Harding's office on wobbly legs. She entered her own office and quickly shut the door.

Thank goodness for Nana Bella. She normally got annoyed when her family interrupted her at work with one of their crazy "emergencies," but this time her dear grandmother had displayed perfect timing. Nana Bella always claimed to be a little psychic—as Italian grandmothers often do, just to keep their children in line— but this episode proved it.

Matt Harding unnerved her enough under normal circumstances—curtly delivering his orders, shouting his displeasure, showing no positive reaction to the many miracles she pulled off. But when he slipped into a personal mode...asking her about her family, her social life—or lack thereof—and praised her work to the sky, she couldn't take it. She'd nearly melted into a puddle of goo, right there on the Persian rug.

What in the world had come over him? Maybe the kitchen had slipped something into his afternoon coffee, she mused.

Sometimes she hated this job. Not her real job, as assistant manager of hotel operations, which she'd started at the Harding Plaza about two months ago. She loved that job. Landing it had been a big step in her career. But this special, temporary assignment. She was never going to make it. She would lose her mind before it was all over.

Why her, of all people? She'd been so happy here at first. Then, just as she was getting her feet wet in the new spot, the buzz spread around the office: Matt Harding needed a temporary replacement for his personal assistant. For some mysterious reason, Stephanie was tapped for the assignment. She couldn't understand it. So many others who were possible choices had been at the hotel far longer. Some of the female managers especially were more than willing—jealously wondering what Stephanie had done to deserve the honor.

But what choice did she have? She couldn't very well refuse. Her boss had presented the call as a real perk—a chance to show off her talents to the top man.

"Do a good job for Mr. Harding and you'll really advance in this organization," her boss had advised her.

Stephanie had a far different view. She'd already heard the lowdown on Matt Harding. For one thing, the dynamic founder of Harding Hotels was reputed to be demanding and temperamental, totally charming one minute, then biting someone's head off the next.

So far she'd barely glimpsed the charming side. The past few weeks had been mostly snarling, barking and a few nips here and there—or totally ignoring her. Which she found most unnerving of all.

Then there was this *other* problem. Matt Harding

himself, an undisputable hunk. With enough masculine magnetism to light up Times Square. When her friends found out she'd been called upon to babysit "His Royal Hotness" they'd had a field day teasing her and giggling endlessly over silly, adolescent fantasies. Stephanie either ignored them, or denied that she felt any attraction.

Nobody believed her. Why would they? He was just *that* good-looking…or something. Stephanie could never quite figure out what it was about Matt Harding that set him apart—she just knew, whatever it was, he had plenty of it.

Yes, secretly she was attracted to him, though she'd never admit it in a million years, not even to her closest friends.

Insanely attracted.

It was insane, Stephanie often reminded herself. And pointless. Like yearning after a movie star or sports figure, some guy so distant and unattainable, he didn't even know you were alive.

Besides, Stephanie knew by now a good relationship was more than a physical attraction. Matthew Harding had his shortcomings. To begin with, he was arrogant, a total egotist, and extremely insensitive. Not the type of man she admired and respected at all. Therefore, no problem. Right?

The kind of man she envisioned settling down with would be solid, sensitive and warm. He would share her values and background. He was not a self-centered playboy, running around with models and actresses half his age. He wanted a wife and family, a real life—and he'd want to make a real and lasting commitment.

The description of her ideal brought to mind her former fiancé, Tommy Torelli. They'd grown up in the same neighborhood of Brooklyn, homey Carroll Gardens. They'd gone to the same schools and had known each other forever. Their parents were friends and Tommy was almost like family.

Stephanie's father had always predicted that one of his daughters would end up a Torelli. But Tommy, in his careful methodical way, took his sweet time making his choice. The summer after Stephanie graduated from college, he asked her out on a date. She'd thought he was joking at first, but when she realized he was serious, Stephanie said, "Sure, why not?"

Maybe that would have been good enough for most people—a comfortable, feet-on-solid-ground start for the same type of clearheaded romance. But it wasn't quite good enough for Stephanie. She wanted more. Some indefinable but essential ingredient was missing. She hadn't noticed it at first, but as time went on, she realized her so-called romance with Tommy never quite progressed beyond, "Sure, why not?"

She might be willing to date a man for that reason, and even go steady for several years. But she ultimately discovered she could not answer his mature and logical proposal of marriage by saying, "Sure, why not?"

Tommy was dear, he was sweet. He had good values, a strong character, an easygoing, pleasant personality. Their backgrounds were so similar, they could share a private joke with a mere glance. But Tommy was not the man she wanted to share her life with.

Her family was shocked and unhappy when Stephanie announced the breakup. Her parents had hoped Angie's wedding would inspire Stephanie to set the date as well. They'd never imagined Angie's nuptials would have just the opposite effect.

"You're throwing away a good chance here, Stephanie," her mother warned. "I just don't understand you sometimes."

Then her father chimed in, "You're just nervous, sweetie. Everybody's afraid to get married, believe me. Sure you like your job. It's fine for a girl to work until the babies come. But you don't want to end up like Aunt Lily, do you? Living alone with a bunch of cats to keep you company?"

Aunt Lily was her grandmother's so-called spinster sister. The story was that when her fiancé died in World War II, Lily would have no other. A spinster or not, Aunt Lily had always seemed very happy and fulfilled to Stephanie. She'd been a schoolteacher and now was active in her retirement years, always traveling to exotic places on educational tours for seniors. Lily always invited Nana Bella to come along, but Stephanie's parents always dissuaded her. Despite her father's dire warning, Aunt Lily's golden years didn't look half bad to Stephanie.

Besides, women had far more choices these days. But try telling that to her well-meaning, but totally sexist, traditional father. He was hardly aware that women had the vote.

What was the use of arguing? Stephanie couldn't explain it. Tommy was a little *too* steady and settled. She wanted to get married, not turn into a zombie.

Only Grandma Bella seemed to understand. "Don't listen to your father. He's not the one marrying Tommy. You did the right thing, sweetheart. Tommy's a nice boy, don't get me wrong. But *figlia bella,* he's not for you," Grandma agreed with a brisk shake of her head. "You need a little…fire."

But who was for her? What faceless stranger would step out of the shadows to inspire that head-over-heels feeling she was holding out for? That breathless rush that reminds a person that life is more than going to work, eating dinner and watching the six-o'clock news? The pure elation and connection of two minds and souls that can fill you with absolute joy?

Who was that man, who would share this adventure with her, Stephanie wondered as she gazed out her office window.

It certainly was *not* Matt Harding.

If she felt he was taking some personal notice of her today, that was merely her overactive imagination. Matt Harding did not look at a woman like her twice. Not when he had the "flavor of the week" supermodels lined up as his Saturday night dates, she reminded herself. All she had to do was open the New York society pages to get dashed with cold water, washing away any misconceptions she might have about his interest in her. Not to mention the hotel grapevine, always ripe for the picking with rumors about her sexy boss's exploits.

There were other rumors too, a sad story about his past. How he'd married his college sweetheart, but she'd broken his heart. According to the gossip, she'd not only left him for another man, but also somehow walked away with the savings he'd planned to use to start his business. He'd been spurned, burned and left with nothing. Somehow, he'd managed to survive those hard times and build his business anyway. But she suspected the scars from that episode went deep. Which might explain his apparent aversion to serious relationships.

But it was not for her to analyze or judge Matt Harding. She wished she didn't think of him at all. He seemed content with his life and happy on his romantic merry-go-round. *I probably make no more impression on him than a new piece of office furniture,* Stephanie thought glumly.

So why did he get so personal today? Maybe he was merely curious, she reasoned. It didn't mean anything at all.

Even if he was feeling some tiny spark of attraction, she couldn't dare encourage it. That would be a total and *complete* disaster. She was in a very vulnerable state right now. She couldn't let her guard down.

She glanced out her office windows at an extraordinary view of Central Park and the uptown skyline, which sparkled with points of light. The moon hung low in a smoky blue sky. Perfectly round and shimmering like a silver coin. Well, maybe that explained it. Nana Bella always warned her about the romantic powers of the full moon, Stephanie thought, smiling to herself.

Perhaps her domineering, gorgeous-but-grouchy boss was not immune to the spell?

Far below, she could see the sidewalks crowded with fast-walking, fast-talking New Yorkers, hurrying home to start their weekend or to meet friends…or meet a date somewhere special. Taxis darted in and out of traffic, and alongside the park entrance, horse-drawn carriages lined up, waiting to take passengers on a romantic moonlit ride.

It was a perfect night to be out in the city. But she had nowhere special to go, no one to meet. It was just as well that she worked late, Stephanie decided. Less time to feel lonely. She wouldn't even bother trying to find another manager. Why ruin someone else's plans, when she had none?

A dash of lipstick and a quick smoothing out of her sedate hairstyle, and she was ready to oversee the journalists' big banquet. Who knows, she mused, as she walked toward the elevators, maybe some dashing international correspondent will sweep me away on his magic trench coat.

Like Nana Bella always said, "When you wake up in the morning, honey, you never know what's going to happen. So make sure you always wear nice underwear, sweetheart. Okay?"

Chapter Two

Matt turned the key and let himself in his front door. A penthouse suite atop the hotel, the luxury apartment was a laughably short commute.

He strolled across the onyx floor of the foyer and into the sweeping living room. He kicked off his shoes, slipped off his suit jacket and yanked off his tie. Then he fixed himself a drink, the usual, bourbon with a splash of soda. Already past seven, he noticed. Not much time left to get ready for his date. The buff-colored leather couch, covered with large suede and Kilim tapestry pillows, looked tempting and he longed to sit back and put his feet up. But Jenna would read him the riot act if he was late. She had pull at the trendiest restaurants and hated to miss out on a good table. A table where she could see all and be seen by all.

At times, she seemed to have no greater joy in life

than finding her blurry photograph in the gossip pages of the morning newspaper. Not his style at all, though so far, he humored her. He'd never courted publicity and actively avoided it. Though the paparazzi always seemed to find him a worthy subject, he couldn't quite understand the fascination. Especially when the gossip columnists put out some absurd story about his private life. But as Jenna often reminded him, any publicity was good publicity. He wasn't so sure about that theory, but never bothered to argue with her.

He took a bolstering swallow of his bourbon and headed for the bedroom, a large master suite. Jenna was not the deepest, most sensitive person he had ever met—but she was very good in bed. Hey, a guy can't expect a woman to be perfect.

Unfortunately, the concept of female perfection brought to mind one woman and one alone...Stephanie Rossi. He stripped off his shirt and trousers, wondering what Stephanie was like in bed. She always seemed so quiet and controlled. Yet he had long suspected that was an act, mostly for his benefit—a "persona" she donned for the office.

For one thing, there was her sense of humor. Surprisingly sharp and even zany at times. And he'd always found you could tell a lot about a woman by watching her eat. One morning he'd spied Stephanie having breakfast at her desk, a sticky cinnamon roll and a frothy cappuccino. The way she had delicately devoured the pastry, her eyes half closed as she licked the tip of one finger, her tongue darting out, skimming the trace of sugary icing....

He felt a lump forming in his throat—and other places on his anatomy—just thinking about it. She was a deeply sensual woman—no question about it. Secretly sensual perhaps. But that would make it all the more delightful to unveil her hidden, erotic side. Yes, a man would be very lucky indeed to be granted that special privilege.

Unlike Jenna, who flaunted her sexuality so boldly he'd become numb to it. Ah, well. Like the song goes, you can't always get what you want.

He strolled across the bedroom in his briefs, not even bothering to glance at his image in the large mirror that hung on the opposite wall. For all his good looks and the admiring glances he constantly received, he was not a vain man. His tall, wide-shouldered frame was lean and fit, with well-developed muscles in his long legs, chest and arms. His chest was covered with a mat of dark brown hair, tapering down his flat, sculpted stomach. He liked to keep fit and needed to be in top shape just to keep up with his demanding lifestyle. He worked out regularly in the hotel's fully equipped health club, and swam laps in the Olympic-size pool. Living across the street from Central Park made it easier to take an early-morning jog, or even go cycling.

Like many men approaching forty, Matt found it wasn't quite as easy to finish those fifty sit-ups, or sprint that last mile. He sometimes worried about going "soft" all over. Yet the truth of the matter was, he didn't have much to worry about. The women in his life never had any complaints.

As Matt pulled a dark-plum bath sheet from the linen closet, he noticed the light flashing on the phone machine, which sat on a writing desk in the corner of the bedroom. He walked over and pressed the answer button.

Jenna's high-pitched voice greeted him. She tended to squeal when excited and he turned the volume down.

"Hey, Matt. It's me. I was really looking forward to seeing you, sweetie. But something has come up at work and I'm leaving tonight for—guess where?—the French countryside. Top secret emergency, sweetie, so don't tell a soul. Guess what? Brian and Melanie are getting married—" Matt frowned. He didn't know any Brian, or Melanie. Then he realized Jenna was talking about two famous actors who were always on the cover of the supermarket tabloids. Brian Bigelow and Melanie Marsh? Something like that.

Jenna, the celebrity authority, often referred to total strangers on a first-name basis, a habit he found annoying.

Jenna's voice rattled on, and he listened with half an ear. He already knew the punch line. He'd been stood up for Brian and Melanie. For some reason, instead of feeling let down, he felt strangely...relieved.

"...so our sources heard the wedding was not going to be in Palm Springs or at Brian's ranch in Montana. I mean, I knew that was a spin all along. Then I found out the *real* location. Brian's stepmother's chateau. She's practically British royalty, you know. Lady Gainsworth...or Gainsworthy? I'm not sure.... Anyway, her personal secretary's sister-in-law goes to the same day spa as I do. So she was getting a body wax in the booth right next to me and I heard everything. Lucky, right?"

How long was his message tape, Matt wondered. Didn't it have an automatic cutoff at some point?

"Sorry, sweetie, but this really is *the* story of the year. I can't miss out. Anyway, kisses and kisses, Matt sweetheart—" Matt heard some juicy kissing sounds and winced a bit. "I'll make it up to you next week. Promise," Jenna added with a sexy laugh.

A long, electronic beep signaled the end of her seemingly endless message. Well, so much for his hot date. He pressed the rewind button on the machine and headed for the shower.

Maybe Jenna breaking this date was in fact, a good thing.

This relationship wasn't going anywhere and it was time he faced it. When she came back, he'd take her out to dinner and have the usual talk. "It's not you, it's me..." etcetera and so on. He knew his lines by heart by now. She'd probably be angry. Maybe even throw a drink at him. Some women did. He'd send her flowers, maybe a nice piece of jewelry?

Was there something wrong with him? Why was he so hard to please? Why couldn't he find a woman who didn't drive him crazy, or just plain bore him to tears?

Matt turned on the shower, adjusted the water to the steaming-hot temperature he preferred, then stepped into the black-marble and glass enclosure. For years, he'd been focused on building his business. Working hard and playing hard. He loved the company of charming, attractive women and was rarely without a gorgeous one in his life. But relationships—real relationships—were never a priority to him. Women seem to come and go, the next one always more enticing than the last.

As a young man, his motto had always been, "So many women, so little time." But now it seemed more as if time was running out, and while he'd enjoyed the company of many, he still hadn't found that special one in the world, the woman that was made just for him. Did she really exist? Would he ever find her?

Once upon a time, he'd been an optimist about such matters. A real romantic. But that had all changed back in college, when his first love left him for another man. She'd not only broken his heart, but had also made off with his inheritance, the seed money for his business. With the help of banks and investors, he'd managed to succeed anyway. Eventually, he'd realized that his ex-wife had robbed him of something even more valuable than money—the courage to reach out and love again.

Now it felt as if he was forever trapped in a hopeless loop of meaningless romances, with trophy dates like Jenna. Finally, just like tonight, he always found himself alone.

He briskly toweled off, then dressed in jeans and a black V-neck pullover. He combed his thick wet hair straight back and didn't even think about shaving. Maybe I'll grow a beard this weekend, he thought as he walked barefoot back into the living room.

He freshened his drink, then flicked on the evening news. The flashing images captured only a fraction of his attention. He was weary and the weekend seemed to stretch out endlessly—echoing with loneliness.

He'd take out his phone book and call someone. There were plenty of names to choose from. He could find a date for tonight, even at such short notice, he consoled himself. He and Jenna didn't really have an exclusive relationship. He considered this solution, then realized there wasn't any other woman he really wanted to see.

Well, there was one. But she was off-limits to him.

He took a gulp of his drink, the ice tinkling against the crystal glass. He'd drive out to his country house and spend the weekend at the beach. Being near the ocean always soothed his nerves and energized him. He'd spend the weekend. Maybe he'd meet somebody new out there, at the shore. Or in a club.

Is that what Stephanie would be doing this weekend? Not spending time with a boyfriend, he knew now. That was some relief. But maybe going out with girlfriends to singles clubs, or on blind dates, trying to find a *new* boyfriend?

He sighed and shifted restlessly in his seat. Why torture yourself? She's clearly and totally off limits. Is that the fascination here? The kind of woman you need is running off to the French countryside to mingle with celebrities. Not hopping a subway to Brooklyn to babysit.

He glanced around the stylishly decorated, perfectly neat apartment. It suddenly felt so sterile…so oppressive. He had to get out of here. He snapped off the TV with the remote and dropped his glass on the marble coffee table.

Back in the bedroom, he started to pack a bag. The phone rang and he paused. Jenna again? Maybe her plans changed and she was free.

He made no move to pick it up. He didn't want to see her tonight after all. The machine answered on the third ring and he listened closely.

"Mr. Harding? I'm sorry to bother you. I'm not even sure if you're there…but a problem has come up that you should know about…."

Stephanie. He leaped toward the writing desk and scooped up the receiver.

"Yes, Stephanie. I'm here. What is it?"

Some glitch with the banquet. She needed his help. He'd run down and smooth it out. Then maybe they'd have dinner together....

"It's Blue Water Cay. Ben Drury, the general manager just called. Talks just broke off with the unions. All the local employees just walked off the job—"

"What!?" Matt jumped up from his seat at the desk.

Blue Water Cay was the newest Harding property, a luxury resort and spa set on a tiny island off Florida's southwest coast. The resort had opened just weeks ago. There were always kinks to work out at a new hotel. He knew the unions were acting up, asking for changes on the contract they'd only just signed. He had a team of mediators and lawyers on it.

But a complete walk-off of all employees? That was a total disaster.

"It was hard to get all the details. You should probably speak to Mr. Drury directly. He's waiting for your call."

"Of course. Do you have his number handy?" Matt grabbed a pen and paper and jotted down the number Stephanie recited.

"Thanks. Don't leave the hotel until you hear from me," he added. "I may need you tonight."

Stephanie promised to wait for his call. She said goodbye and hung up.

Matt quickly dialed the general manager of Blue Water Cay Resort. The phone rang once and Ben's voice came on the line.

"What the hell is going on down there?" Matt began the conversation without bothering with a greeting. "My assistant says you just had a full-scale walkout."

Ben confirmed the bad news and went on to explain

the problem in detail. Beneath his calm tone, Matt could sense that the newly promoted general manager was indeed, in a panic.

Understandably. It was a mess few hoteliers would ever have to face. Yet Matt was still angry that the situation had gone so far out of control before anyone had called him.

"The worst news is the union reps have walked out of their meetings with our representatives. Unfortunately, guests are starting to walk out, too."

Just what he didn't want to hear. An incident like this could tarnish the new hotel's reputation for years to come. Matt simply couldn't let this happen.

"Enough said. I've got the picture." Matt considered reading Ben Drury the riot act. Then realized that would only waste time. Once he reached the hotel, he'd have plenty of opportunity to reprimand his top executive.

"Hold tight. I'll be there in a few hours." Matt glanced at his watch. "I'll call from Miami. Send a car to the airport."

The trip to the island from New York required a flight to Miami and then a puddle jumper, a small twin-engine plane that made quick runs to the islands.

"Sure thing. It might be hard to catch a shuttle tonight, though. You may have to wait until morning," Ben advised in a nervous tone.

"I'll be there tonight. One way or another," Matt promised him.

Sounding like a man about to face the guillotine, Drury said goodbye quickly and hung up.

And with good reason. There was a major mess to be cleaned up, and he was the only one able to do it.

Along with Stephanie Rossi, he silently added.

The thought struck like an inspiration. He couldn't think of anyone at this moment more able to help him. He was sure of it. She had to come. He'd make her come. He wouldn't give her any choice.

You just want to see her in a bathing suit, his chiding voice cut in.

That's not it at all. I need help down there. I can't do it all on my own. She's terrific at handling disgruntled guests, figuring out staffing, everything that needs to be covered to run a hotel.

Okay...I would love to see her in a bathing suit. With one of those matching sarong things floating around her hips, he mused.

But that's totally beside the point!

Packing his bag with one hand, he dialed Stephanie with the other and then tucked the phone between his shoulder and cheek.

"I just spoke to Drury. It's a disaster. I'm going down there right away."

"Oh...that's too bad," Stephanie murmured in agreement. He could hear the banquet in the background. The clatter of plates and the murmur of the partying journalists.

"Who's at the concierge desk tonight?"

"Max," Stephanie replied.

"Have him book two seats on the next flight to Miami. If he can't find a connection to the Cay tonight, have him hire a private plane. Something small. Then meet me in the lobby in fifteen minutes. I need you to come along. Got that?"

He waited for her reply, hearing only silence. He imagined the shocked look on her lovely face.

"I'm sorry…it's a little noisy in here. Did you say you want me to come to Blue Water Cay?"

"That's what I said. You're my assistant, aren't you?" he reminded her. "Isn't an assistant expected to *assist* with emergencies?"

He felt a twinge of conscience at his gruff sarcasm.

He wasn't really annoyed, just trying to strong-arm her into a quick agreement. If she didn't fear her job was on the line, he reasoned, she might make some excuse not to go.

"Why…yes. I mean, of course. I just didn't expect…" Stephanie paused and took a deep breath. "I don't have any clothes. Or even a toothbrush. Maybe I should run up to my apartment and pack a bag."

"Sorry. No time. You can buy a toothbrush and whatever you need at the resort. Just put it on an expense account. Any other questions?"

"Uh…no. Okay," she said finally. "I'll see you in the lobby in fifteen minutes."

He hung up the phone and rubbed his face with his hands. Suddenly, he wondered if taking Stephanie Rossi with him was such a great idea after all.

"Whisked away! To a tropical paradise!"

That's what Nana Bella's reaction had been. Nana was the only family Stephanie had been able to reach while she waited in the lobby for her boss to appear. She knew they'd be looking for her over the weekend, maybe even call the police when she didn't answer her phone messages. It was wiser by far simply to tell someone what was happening.

But her grandmother, bless her soul, hadn't understood at all that this was hardly a pleasure trip and that her impossible boss probably expected her to body-block an entire herd of stampeding guests heading for the checkout desk. Among other impossible feats.

Nana didn't get any of that. When she heard the news, she shouted, "Whoopee! You're being whisked away to a tropical island! Just like Desiree and Chad...."

Desiree and Chad were Nana's favorite characters from her favorite soap opera *Tempest Rock*. Since Nana's world beyond the Rossi household was limited, the soap had become her primary point of reference and she often confused the events on *Tempest Rock* with real life.

"This is just business, Nana. A real emergency," Stephanie explained.

The most miserable forty-eight hours of her life, most likely. Stephanie considered cooking up some last-minute excuse. Could she suddenly remember some crucial doctor's appointment? Or some family crisis?

He'll never believe me, she thought.

The moment to wriggle out of this invitation had passed. He hadn't even given her a moment. She felt as if a gun had been held to her head, the unspoken threat being, "Come along...or else."

"Believe me, I'm not being...*whisked* in any way, Nana. Hijacked is more like it."

"I've seen pictures of your boss, sweetheart. I'd let that guy whisk me—or hijack me, even—in a heartbeat...."

"Nana...don't be silly." Stephanie felt her cheeks flush. Nana had a point. A fairly irrefutable one.

Stephanie felt someone standing beside her and

looked up to find Matt. She wondered how long he'd been standing there. How much he'd overheard.

"So long, Nana. I've got to run—"

"Have a good trip, sweetheart. I'm going to light a candle for you!" Nana called happily after her.

Stephanie said goodbye again, clicked off her phone and stashed it in her purse.

"Checking in with your family?" His tone was bland but a faint light of amusement danced in his dark eyes.

"I needed to call in case anyone was looking for me."

"Very thoughtful…and don't worry about Sunday dinner. I'll write you a note."

She felt annoyed at his teasing for a moment. But his warm smile quickly melted her anger. Practically melted her bones, she realized. She found it hard enough to deal with him when he was being bossy and demanding. When he got all up close and personal like this, it was truly a challenge.

That's the last time I'll tell him anything about my real life, she vowed.

"I've got the e-tickets from Max. The flight leaves in about an hour and half, which should give us plenty of time. The car is out front, waiting," she recited efficiently.

"Good work." He smiled again, making her heart skip a beat. She'd never seen him dressed before in casual clothes. His worn denim jeans hung low on his hips, draping his long legs like an advertisement for male sex appeal. A soft black pullover, with the sleeves pushed up his forearms, molded his physique, emphasizing wide shoulders, a hard chest and washboard abs.

He wore it without a T-shirt underneath and the high V-neck tantalized with a hint of dark chest hair.

He bent to pick up his duffel bag and she remembered again that she was traveling light. Frighteningly light.

What kind of clothes would she find at a resort shop on a tropical island—batik wrap skirts and tie-dyed bikinis?

Well, one disaster at a time, she coached herself.

Chapter Three

It all felt very dreamlike, Stephanie thought later. As if she and Matt were in a movie. The speeding ride to the airport in a long black limo. Their mad dash to the gate. The VIP treatment by the airline personnel.

She'd barely fastened her seat belt and caught her breath when the plane began to take off. She'd never sat in first class before. She had to admit, it wasn't so bad. The leather seats were soft and roomy and tilted back for dozing. Like sitting in her Dad's new deluxe La-Z-Boy recliner. She and her sisters had chipped in on Father's Day and bought him the top-of-the-line model, complete with back massaging action at the touch of a button.

Of course, when you compared the two seating situations, you had to factor in proximity to Matt Harding. Though Stephanie wasn't sure if that went in the plus or minus column.

She snuck a quick glance at her boss, who sat disturbingly close. He reached into his pocket and pulled out a pack of gum, unwrapped a stick and stuck it in his mouth. Then turned and offered her some.

"Helps relieve the air pressure when you take off," he promised.

She shook her head. "No thanks. I'm fine."

He shrugged and stuck the gum back in his pocket. Staring straight ahead, he seemed to be thinking. Then he did the most amazing thing. The last thing she'd ever expect of him.

He blew a huge pink bubble.

Stephanie watched him, her mouth falling open. It grew and grew to an enormous, hypnotizing size. Then he somehow pulled the entire thing into his mouth and smashed it, with a loud pop.

He turned to her with a coaxing smile. "Sure you don't want some? We could have a contest."

"A contest?"

"See who can blow the biggest bubble," he said, seeming surprised she didn't understand.

She couldn't tell from his tone if he was teasing her again. It seemed as if he might be. She'd rarely seen this playful side. She didn't quite know how to react.

Retreat! Retreat! Run like...heck, a secret voice advised her. You don't want to encourage this man, Stephanie. He's out of your league, believe me. And bubble gum isn't good for your teeth.

"I brought some files about the resort. I thought I'd look them over. Try to get some ideas of how to keep things going without a full staff...."

His playful expression took on a more serious cast. "Of course. Very efficient of you, Stephanie. As always."

He sighed and dug down into his briefcase. "I brought some, too." He pulled out a wad of files and a laptop computer. "Maybe we can figure out some strategies."

Stephanie agreed, relieved to see him switch back into "boss" mode again. She swallowed hard. She didn't want to get personal with him. But traveling and working together all weekend like this was going to be a challenge.

But once she and Matt got down to work, the time passed quickly and the flight to Miami wasn't nearly as difficult as she'd expected. She actually enjoyed brainstorming with him, and he always seemed very interested in her perspective. He knew so much and was very creative for a businessman, she thought. She learned a lot, just trading ideas with him.

He's not just a pretty face, she thought with a secret smile.

When they reached Miami, they quickly found their connection, a small, local airline that flew between the mainland and many islands. The flight was not on the regular schedule, but since Matt was willing to pay handsomely for all sixteen seats, the pilot was willing to take him wherever he wanted to go.

Stephanie was not the greatest flyer and felt a little wary of the tiny, noisy aircraft. She took a seat and fastened her belt, forcing a calm expression.

Matt sat down beside her and patted her hand. "Nothing to worry about. We'll be up and down before you even know it.'

She turned to him, feeling even more distressed. "That's exactly what I was thinking."

He smiled, but in a way that didn't make her foolish. More like her burgeoning hysteria was somehow…cute.

"Sure you don't want some gum?" he asked in a kind voice. "It might distract you."

He took out the pack again and held it out to her. This time she took a stick. "Thanks."

"No problem. I'll let you warm up a little. Then we'll let the games begin."

She glanced at him, wondering if he was serious. He did look serious. She looked straight ahead, smiling a little. "I need to warn you. I grew up in Brooklyn. Four sisters. I'm tough."

"Bring it on, babe." He glanced at her, nearly laughing and she felt her smile growing even wider. Then she held her hand out for the pack of gum again.

"Two sticks each. Best three out of five."

He looked surprised yet pleased at her challenging tone. "You're on."

Stephanie took the second stick of gum and started to chew. Then tried to remember how to blow a bubble. It had been a long time….

The rickety, noisy twin-engine plane rolled down the runway and slowly rose in the air without her barely noticing. When she looked out the window, they were flying smoothly over water and she could already see their destination, the small green island, nearby.

Matt won the bubble-blowing contest easily. His efforts were amazing. Her first two were laughable, but her last one was a real contender.

"You're good," she admitted as the plane taxied down the runway. "Who would have guessed this hidden talent?"

He grinned at her, looking pleased by the compliment. "There are a lot of things you don't know about me, Stephanie. You'd be surprised."

His dark eyes flashed a silent challenge. She met his gaze a minute and looked away.

If I didn't know better, I'd swear he's flirting with me. Maybe Nana was right. Maybe I am getting whisked.

Stephanie turned her head and gave herself a mental shake. *She was imagining this, right? Or maybe he was flirting, but it didn't mean anything. He was bored and just flexing some cramped male flirting muscles. Just wants to make sure everything is in working order. Sort of like testing a fire alarm?*

She wondered where she'd find his reset button. She *really* needed to turn it off.

Another sleek limo met them at Blue Cay's tiny airport and they rode the short distance to the hotel without speaking much. The air-conditioned car sped down an empty, narrow road, and the dark and tropical night surrounded them. Palm trees on the roadside swayed gently and the deep-blue sky above was studded with white stars. She couldn't see the water but sensed it all around, the scent of the sea in the heavy humid air like a strange perfume.

The limo turned down a long driveway that led to the resort. The columned entrance and portico was brightly lit and very impressive, everything white with blue tile. The surrounding landscape gave the impression of a lush rainforest, with giant Royal Palms and masses of tropical plants and colorful flowers,

She stepped out of the car and stared around, feeling very disoriented. And instantly sticky and overdressed, even in her spring weight suit. She could actually feel her hair curling in the humidity, springing loose from the pins that held it in place. She felt rumpled and tired and knew that she must look a dreadful mess.

Matt sprang out of the car, seeming energized and in total control. "Finally," he said. He took her arm and began to lead her towards the lobby.

The hotel looked quiet, especially for a Friday night she thought. Then she realized, no bellmen, rushing forward to take their bags and help them check in. One lonely soul standing at the front desk.

The lone employee behind the desk spotted their approach and rushed toward them, flying through the automatic glass doors.

"Mr. Harding…. How was your trip? Here, let me take that for you." Ben Drury, the hotel general manager, Stephanie guessed.

And I thought I've had a bad day. His was just beginning.

Ben Drury made a grab for Matt's leather duffel bag, but Matt held on firmly.

"That's all right, Ben. I can handle it." He cast his employee a tight smile.

Ben backed off, still smiling, looking as if he might very well stumble over his own feet. He was that nervous.

"As you like. If you need a hand, just holler."

"This is my assistant, Stephanie Rossi. She's come down to help out."

Matt stepped aside to make the introductions and Ben shook Stephanie's hand. "Pleased to meet you, Ms. Rossi. Welcome. If you need anything at all while you're here—"

I'd better get it myself. Because there's no one left working here, Stephanie silently finished for him. She glanced at Matt, sensing he knew what she was thinking and shared the joke. It was a struggle to keep a straight face as Ben completed his welcoming speech.

"—just let me know. I'd be delighted to help you in any way possible...."

Still, Stephanie felt awfully sorry for the guy. The disaster wasn't exactly his fault. Though he might lose his job over it. She smiled at him. "Thank you," she said quietly.

"You must be tired from the trip. Would you like to see your rooms? I've booked you both in the beachfront suites. I think you'll be quite comfortable."

That sounded like a plan, Stephanie thought. She was exhausted. She definitely wanted to see her room. Particularly, her pillow.

But Matt seemed to have some other plan in mind. She could tell from the way he frowned at the suggestion, before he'd even spoken a word.

"We didn't come down here to sleep, Drury. I need a full update on the property. What kind of staff are we left with, what's the occupancy? What's going on with the union talks?"

Matt's voice rose a notch on each point. Ben Drury seemed to flinch inside his dark blue suit.

Stephanie felt instantly jolted awake. She took a deep breath and glanced at Drury. He was in the hot seat and she felt sorry for him all over again.

She suddenly felt sorry for herself, too. It looked as if they were going to be up all night.

Up all night with Matthew Harding. Was her name going to be added to some long list in his diary, she joked to herself. With a footnote, of course.

How could hell look so much like paradise?

That was Stephanie's first thought as she stepped through the glass doors and stared out at the magnificent view. The private patio, complete with a pool and hot tub, was set right on the beach, steps from the crystal blue bay. At half past six in the morning, the beach was totally empty, serene in the early light. The sand looked fine and white as sugar and the sea was a crystal shade of turquoise blue.

The private patio was beautifully landscaped, with scarlet and white hibiscus and hot-pink bougainvillea that bloomed wildly while tall palms provided corners of shade. A lattice-work wall, covered with a lush, flowering vine separated the space from the neighboring suite.

The suite where her boss was presumably still sleeping.

Stephanie hugged the hotel-issue, terry-cloth bathrobe around her slim form and padded back inside. She wasn't even sure how she'd woken up so early. The alarm clock she'd found on the nightstand had helped. And she never could sleep late in a strange place.

But it was mostly sheer terror that had propelled her out of bed today, after little more than four hours' sleep.

She pulled apart the little coffeemaker in the suite's efficient kitchen. She set it up and turned it on. Coffee. She needed some. Bad. Real bad. Though she must have drunk at least a gallon of it last night.

They'd worked until nearly 2:00 a.m., Ben Drury,

Matt, Stephanie and a few key executives, huddled together as they reviewed every facet of hotel operations. Hotel in-operations was more like it—as in totally inoperative, out of order, defunct.

This was not a surprise. The surprise was that Matt—bullheaded, optimistic, never say die—Harding expected to keep things up and running until the labor dispute was resolved. Which, at the current rate, looked like never.

Stephanie had to admire him. Another man would have closed the place down, booked the guests into other hotels, the Harding resort in the Florida Keys for instance. Or sent them home with rain checks or gift certificates. But not Matt Harding.

Pushed to the wall—and delirious from sleep deprivation and an overdose of caffeine—Stephanie had come up with a few innovative ideas last night that seemed to both impress and please her boss.

But it was one thing to come up with these crazy tactics to keep guests happy and fed and so full of blender drinks, they couldn't budge off their lounge chairs, much less pack up and leave the place early.

It was another story entirely to actually pull the rabbit out of the hat. To pull off these crowd-pleasing tricks.

She'd left with the other executives, while Matt remained, going over the union contract with a bleary-eyed Drury.

Matt had hardly seemed tired, she recalled, while the rest of them were sitting with their chins on the table. He had stamina. Loads of it. The gossip about him was true. He could go all night. She smiled into her mug as the errant image raced through her mind.

The sound of splashing water broke into her

thoughts. She returned to the glass doors again and glanced at the pool, expecting to see a seagull looking for a luxury bird bath. The pool was empty, without a ripple. Then she realized the sound was coming from next door. Matt's territory.

She took a few quiet steps outside and peeked through the vine-covered divider. She could see his dark head cutting through the surface of the water, his long muscular arms and smooth broad back glistening as he made his way down the length of the pool with a powerful breaststroke.

He was…gorgeous. No question. He looked good in clothes, but this was something else altogether.

She felt guilty watching him in secret, a peeping Tom. Or the female equivalent. Still, she couldn't force herself to look away. He was the very definition of total hunk. The masculine ideal. His torso rose as he reached forward in the water and her gaze slid down his sleek form….

What a pair of shoulders. Look at those arms. What a cute butt….

He twisted onto his back, floating a moment as he stared at the sky, then started a backstroke.

Her gaze scanned the flip side, from head to—

Stephanie blinked and dropped her mug. It crashed and broke into a million pieces. She jumped out of the way with a muffled curse, hot coffee burning her toes. She glanced through the screen just long enough to see that Matt had indeed heard the noise and knew she was standing there.

She heard the splashing stop and didn't dare look again to see if he was coming out of the pool.

"Stephanie? Is that you?"

It's my evil twin. I would never stand here, stalking you. Gawking at your naked anatomy...

Feeling totally mortified, her cheeks flaming as if she'd sat all day in the sun, she swiftly crept inside, not daring to make a sound.

Her only hope was to avoid Matt when he left his room, she decided.

She quickly dressed in her rinsed-out underwear and yesterday's outfit. Then twisted up her hair and brushed her teeth with the corner of a washcloth and the complimentary toothpaste.

No makeup to hide the bags under her eyes. She could only find a tube of lipstick in her purse. The wrong color, but she put it on anyway, then checked herself out in the mirror.

She looked terrible. No question.

There are worse ways to start the day, Stephanie, she reminded herself. Like being caught checking out your boss in his birthday suit.

Stephanie arrived at the main building of the hotel feeling breathless. Luckily, there was a plan, outlined last night at the meeting. The first hurdle was getting through breakfast service. Stephanie found every able-bodied employee of the hotel assembled in the kitchen, with most not having the faintest idea of what to do.

She checked her notes and got them moving, somehow setting up a passable breakfast buffet in the outdoor dining space. Ben Drury, wearing a chef's hat and apron, manned the omelet station.

The poor man was desperate to save his job, Stephanie realized. He'd do just about anything, short of posing on a platter with an apple in his mouth. He'd been trained in the food and beverage area of the hotel before his promotions, she'd learned, so this was a logical and the most helpful place for him to stay all day.

Out in the dining room, a man in a golf cap complained at the self-service concept. His grumbling was nearly as loud as the print on his Hawaiian shirt.

"A buffet? Give me a frigging break. I'm paying good money to have a waiter carry my food to the table. Didn't the rest of you?"

A few guests averted their gaze, too polite to engage him. But some others started ranting, too.

Not even nine o'clock and she was facing a mutiny.

Drury rushed around, playing waiter in an attempt to placate them. Stephanie ran over and poured out coffee. Then talked up the freebies that would be available today in all parts of the hotel—free tennis lessons, sailboats, Jet Skis and down in the spa, massages, facials and aromatherapy.

The frowns soon turned to smiles while Stephanie made a mental note to have a huge sign posting the free services placed at the front desk—giving second thoughts to anyone trying to check out.

The rebellion had been quelled. Momentarily. Stephanie sighed, her body sagging with relief. Would she ever manage to last the day?

"How are you doing, Stephanie? Everything under control?"

Matt's voice put her on instant alert. She felt as if he'd just materialized beside her out of thin air. Like a character on *Star Trek*.

She stood up tall and forced a smile. "So far, so good. We got the breakfast service going and the complimentary spa treatments and water sports vouchers seem to be working."

"Yes, a great idea. That should help." Matt was dressed in fresh clothes, she noticed. A blue shirt, black pants and a charcoal-gray linen jacket and silk tie. His crisp attire made her feel even more crumpled. She made a mental note to check out the resort shops at some point, if she could.

As good as he looked in his outfit, she couldn't help but remember what was underneath....

"Up early?"

"Um...yes. I was. I got up early and headed right over here."

Liar, liar. Pants on fire, she chided herself.

"Really? What a shame. It was a beautiful morning. You should have taken a few minutes out on your patio. To check out the view."

Stephanie felt her cheeks flame, but forced herself to keep a calm expression.

He knew. He just enjoyed playing games, didn't he?

She looked up and met his eye. "I was in a rush today. Maybe tomorrow morning," she answered smoothly, "when I have more time to enjoy it."

His bland expression changed suddenly, looking surprised at her comeback.

I grew up in Brooklyn, pal. I already warned you, she added silently.

"I have some good news," he said, changing the subject. "Some reinforcements from our hotels in Boca Raton and the Keys are flying in this morning to help out. You're in charge of figuring out how to use them. I don't even trust Drury to make toast, quite frankly," Matt added, glancing over his shoulder.

The assignment and authority he'd just given her was a great compliment. Stephanie felt honored...and overwhelmed, but tried to stay cool.

"The priority right now is housekeeping. I guess I'll put most of the helpers to work there and see how it goes."

"Good strategy. I'll be in meetings with the union reps all day. If you need me, send a message and I'll get back to you." Matt smiled at her. "Good luck."

She smiled back, feeling suddenly close to him. "Good luck to you, too. I hope it goes well."

"Cross your fingers. The sooner we can sort this all out, the sooner we get to go back to New York."

Which couldn't be soon enough for me, Stephanie thought. She forced a smile as he nodded and walked over to chat with Ben Drury. She couldn't help but notice the women in the dining room, forks poised midway to their mouths as they checked Matt out.

If the guests really get restless, we can always have Matt swim laps in the hotel pool. That will at least keep the ladies away from the checkout desk.

Somewhat cheered by the news of more employees on the way, Stephanie headed for the lobby, her pad of strategy notes tucked under one arm. The assistant manager of accounting was manning the front desk. Stephanie was almost sure that Shirley Conrad didn't have the foggiest idea of what she was doing, but at least she had shown up for work this morning and was trying her best.

"How's it going?" Stephanie asked her.

"Pretty quiet. A few couples asked me about flights off the island today, but so far, nobody's checked out early."

"I think they're all still getting their fill of the free breakfast. Let's hope all the carbs make them want to nap."

"If the pancakes don't work, try some piña coladas."

"Excellent suggestion. Happy Hour may start a little early today. Like in about…fifteen minutes."

Shirley giggled. "Rev up the blenders. Anything for the cause."

"That's the spirit." Stephanie smiled as she slipped behind the desk to check the registration activity. The front desk had been quiet, just as Shirley reported. A good sign. Though it was still early yet.

She heard the sound of arguing, more like low-level hissing and looked up to see a man and woman loaded down with suitcases, golf clubs and tote bags as they stumbled across the lobby.

"Our first customers. Let's see if we can get them to stay," she whispered to Shirley.

The two women ran out from behind the desk and approached the couple. "Here, let us help you with those bags," Stephanie said smoothly. She grabbed a suitcase in each hand and soon had it placed on the bell cart Shirley rolled over.

"We're checking out. The reservation is under the name Ames, Harold and Alice. We were supposed to stay to Tuesday, but we're checking out," the man said belligerently. He dumped his golf clubs on the cart with a deafening rattle. "I have a good mind to ask for my money back on the days we spent here, too."

"Harold…please." The woman tugged his sleeve. "It wasn't *that* bad…."

"Now you just let me handle this, Alice. I'm not paying for 'not that bad.' I'm paying for deluxe. And I certainly didn't get it. Not once the help walked off."

"We came here for our anniversary. Thirty years," the wife explained. Stephanie thought she saw the woman glance at her spouse and roll her eyes, which Stephanie read as the universal sign of disbelief that she'd lasted so long in her marriage.

"Thirty years? Congratulations," Stephanie crooned. "That's really an achievement. If only we'd known you were celebrating such a big event, Mr. Ames. I would have been happy to upgrade you to one of our VIP suites. Very lovely. A private pool and Jacuzzi. Private beachfront, too. Did you get the champagne dinner or the his and hers massages at the spa?"

She knew very well that Harold and Alice had not been given any of these perks and upgrades, and watched as Alice turned to her husband with a shocked expression.

"Harold…a beachfront suite. Free massages…"

"I heard. I heard." He frowned, looking uncomfortable as he considered how foolish he might look, giving up his belligerent stance. "You'd do all that for us? Gratis, I mean?"

Stephanie shrugged. "Our gift to you. In honor of your anniversary."

Harold glanced at Alice, who gave her husband a mournful look. "All right," he said finally. "My wife wants to stay longer, so I guess we'll stick it out."

Stephanie nearly laughed at his self-sacrificing tone. She'd just agreed to hundreds of dollars of complimentary charges. It was a lot for free. But Stephanie knew that if one guest had a bad time at the hotel, they would go back home and tell ten others, and that would be thousands of dollars in business lost. But if they were pleased with their stay, that would translate to more new business.

"I think you'll be very comfortable in your suite and if you need anything at all to make your stay more enjoyable, just let me know," Stephanie added.

Shirley had already gone behind the desk and scanned the computer for an unoccupied suite that was ready for a check-in.

"We can put you in room 505. Just give me a minute and I'll make the keys."

"Don't worry about the luggage," Stephanie added. "I'll find someone to bring it down to the room for you."

Probably yours truly, she added silently.

"And don't forget to check out all the complimentary services the hotel is offering this weekend—water sports, golf, tennis and spa treatments."

"Golf? That sounds good to me," Harold chuckled.

"I always wanted to try a seaweed wrap. They say it's marvelous for your skin. I'm going to run down there right now, before the rush." Alice kissed her husband on the cheek and trotted off toward the spa.

Harold collected his new key and pulled his golf clubs off the luggage cart. "Thanks for your help, miss," he said to Stephanie. "See you around."

With a cheerful, jaunty walk, he was off to the greens. Stephanie turned to Shirley and they joined in a long, relieved sigh. Shirley stuck out her hand and Stephanie shook it.

"Nice work."

"Thanks, you too," Stephanie replied.

"Yes, very nice work, ladies." Matt appeared, coming out from an office door behind the reception desk.

Stephanie realized he must have been there all along, listening in to the exchange. Shirley looked surprised, then terrified, suddenly bowing her head and tapping away like mad on the computer keyboard.

Stephanie faced him. "It's not nice to spy on people."

"I wasn't spying...and look who's talking," he replied, his eyebrows jumping up a notch.

She knew he was talking about his morning swim again.

She felt a blush creep up her neck and took a steadying breath.

Before she could frame a proper answer, Matt brushed by her and headed for the luggage cart.

"Are you taking that to the storage room?" Stephanie asked.

"I'm taking it to room 505," he answered, pushing the cart with both hands. "Your talents are obviously needed here, on the battlefront."

Stephanie was surprised to see him pitch in in such hands-on style. But he did seem like a hands-on type of guy, she noted. A good thing...and a bad thing. Though he'd so far never tried to get his hands on her, she was starting to have the oddest feeling it was just a matter of time.

She watched him push the cart away, putting his strong back and long legs into the job. She wondered how he'd ever gotten started in the hotel business and decided to ask him someday. She had a feeling it was an interesting story.

He was an interesting man. An unusual man. A dynamic personality and yet, with a gentle, charming side, too.

She respected him, she realized. Otherwise, she'd never be able to take all his guff.

But I'm not going to get involved with him, she added firmly, catching herself. No matter how much he flirts with me. Really...I'm just not.

Chapter Four

"Look...a van from the airport just pulled up. Oh, God. I hope it isn't more guests!"

Stephanie nearly laughed out loud at Helen's expression. it was the first time she'd ever seen a desk clerk terrified by approaching guests.

"Just take a deep breath. We'll get through this."

Stephanie walked across the lobby and then outside toward the van, which was now parked. The door opened and the passengers began emptying out.

A woman in a neat tan business suit approached and held out her hand. Stephanie spied the gold name tag on her lapel and recognized another Harding hotel employee.

She sighed with relief. The reinforcements had arrived.

She greeted each of them as they emerged, then led the group into the hotel for a quick meeting. She explained the situation and the plan to keep the guests happy that had been worked out the night before.

Everyone seemed very professional and eager to help in any way they could. There were only a dozen more bodies to put to work, but every pair of hands helped.

Stephanie gave them each assignments and they headed off in all directions. A short time later, another van of Harding employees arrived and she did the same.

At noon, she checked on the lunch service, another buffet, set up at the pool. Ben Drury decided to fire up the barbecue and wearing his chef's hat again, happily flipped burgers, hot dogs, shrimp on skewers and grilled chicken breasts. The guests seemed content with the offerings.

Shirley reported that the front desk had checked out a few guests, but nothing extreme. Many seemed occupied on the beach and at the spa. The tactics to keep occupancy up seemed to be working, but just for a little insurance, Stephanie decided to take Helen's advice and opened the beachfront bar with free blender drinks for all.

Then she called up the band that usually played Saturday night in the lounge, performing a mix of pop tunes and Caribbean sound. She asked them to come over immediately and start early, at the poolside. The group was happy to get the extra work.

The afternoon wore on. The makeshift housekeeping crew managed to get all the rooms in order. The makeshift kitchen staff managed to move from one meal to the next without too many problems. The day was passing quickly and Stephanie ran from crisis to crisis. Sticking her finger in one leak, as another sprang out somewhere else on the boat.

By some miracle, the hotel was up and operating with its makeshift staff. Though just barely. But all the guests seemed to be having a good time and hardly noticed.

That was some achievement, she thought.

But Nana did light a candle for me, she recalled.

She hadn't seen Matt all day and guessed he was closed up in meetings. Which was just as well, since she didn't like the idea of him spying on her, the way he had this morning. Especially while she was racing around in "insane mode."

It was nearly seven o'clock when she finally sat down. She chose a quiet corner in the kitchen and sipped a diet soda. Her feet were aching, but she didn't dare remove her sensible pumps, for fear of never getting them back on again.

"How are you holding up, Stephanie?" Ben walked over to her. He'd been working in the kitchen all day but seemed cheerful. He'd taken off his tall chef's hat but still wore an apron.

"I'm good. As soon as this is over I'm getting a foot massage," she added. "What the heck, I'll get my entire body done."

Ben laughed. "You go for it. You deserve it."

"My sentiments exactly." Matt suddenly appeared behind Ben and came to stand between them.

From the way he was looking at her she thought Mr. Hands-on was going to offer to do the job himself.

You wish, dear, a little voice chided.

"I just checked the computer at the front desk. Very few early checkouts today. Much less than we expected. You did a good job. Both of you," he said, glancing from Ben back to Stephanie.

Stephanie held his gaze for a moment, then looked away, feeling her bones starting to melt.

"I think most of the guests were just too tired or distracted to leave," she said finally. "They were either wiped out from taking advantage of all the free sports activities. Or the free food and cocktails. Or just so mellow from the spa, nobody was complaining."

Matt laughed. "I peeked out the window at about five o'clock. They were all on lounge chairs, sleeping off the freebies. It looked like naptime in a kindergarten class."

Stephanie shrugged. "A little underhanded maybe. But it worked."

"Come on now, it was more than freebies," Ben said enthusiastically. "I don't think we would have made it through the day without Stephanie. That girl can think on her feet."

Stephanie thought his compliment was very generous. Considering that he was still in danger of losing his job. A lot of other executives in his position would have hogged all the credit for themselves.

"Ben did a terrific job with the meal service. That was key. If they weren't happy with the food, they wouldn't have stayed. And he's made such a great barbecue out there tonight. It's quite a party."

"Thanks, Stephanie. That's nice of you to say." He glanced her way and then over at Matt.

"So I noticed. Everyone seems very satisfied. Good job, Ben."

"Thank you, sir." Ben seemed surprised at Matt's compliment…and very pleased, she thought.

Stephanie had a sudden inspiration. Instead of firing Ben, maybe Matt should move him back to food and beverage. He seemed very comfortable and happy in that role and might welcome less pressure.

As head of the department, he'd still have a good title and authority. It wouldn't be a total comedown for him. He was a hard worker and loved the hotel. Stephanie hoped Matt would consider the idea. She liked Ben and wanted to help him in some way if she could.

"I have good news," Matt announced. "The unions have accepted a revised contract and the staff will begin reporting back to work right away, starting midnight."

Stephanie's mouth dropped open in surprise. "That's terrific." She sighed and pressed her hand to her chest. "Thank goodness. I don't know how long I could have lasted at this pace."

"That's great news. Thank you, Matt." Ben took Matt's hand and pumped it happily. "I'm going to spread the word. I think it will give everyone a real boost."

Ben quickly headed off to the other side of the kitchen and Stephanie was left alone with Matt. His dark, appraising gaze seemed to focus on her, like a laser beam. She liked it much better when he was being belligerent and unreasonable. Giving her no more notice than a piece of furniture.

This thoughtful, attentive mode threw her off entirely.

"So, how are those feet? As bad as you say?"

"I'll make it. Especially now that I know the worst is over."

"Ben was right. You held the place together today, Stephanie. I'm very impressed." Stephanie met his gaze but didn't know what to say. He was looking at her in a distinctly unnerving way. As if he'd never seen her before. Or had seen her, but she now looked different to him.

"You take the rest of the night off. Why don't you have that massage you were taking about?"

"I think the spa is closed now, isn't it?"

"I'll tell them to open for you. Or you could have it right in your room."

The thought was tempting. But Stephanie still felt the need to decline.

"Thanks, but I think I'll pass. Once I'm in a horizontal position, I have a feeling I'd conk out in a second. I'd like to be awake enough to enjoy it."

"That's a consideration, I guess." Matt slowly smiled, and she realized that her excuse could rule out any number of evening activities.

"You must be hungry though. How about some dinner?"

"With you, you mean?"

The inane reply just flew out, her tongue working faster than her brain. She was so tired, it was hard to hide her surprise.

Matt laughed. "Yes, I meant with me. Would that be all right with you? It's nicer having company than eating alone, don't you think?"

His question wasn't challenging or snide, more curious sounding. As if he really wasn't sure she found his company appealing.

"Oh…sure. That sounds fine," she said lightly. She met his gaze, then looked away, feeling suddenly self-conscious.

He glanced at his watch. "I have a few calls to make. Why don't I meet you out at the bar on the beach in about…ten minutes?"

Stephanie nodded. "That sounds fine."

At least she would have some time to freshen up. No

chance of changing her rumpled outfit, but maybe she could find some makeup in the gift shop?

Get a grip, Stephanie. You worked your tail off today and he feels sorry for you, so he asked you to have a bite of dinner with him. You're not Cinderella heading off to the ball.

Fine. But would a real toothbrush be asking too much? Stephanie argued back to her sensible side. Hey, I'm just going for basic hygiene here…and maybe a tube of mascara.

Twenty minutes later, Stephanie sat at the beach bar, sipping a frosty Cosmopolitan. She'd broken the speed record for freshening up her appearance and had even managed to fit in a quick shopping trip at a resort shop in the lobby.

She'd scooped up a toothbrush, mascara, concealer and a lipstick called Provocative Pink. She usually didn't wear such bright colors, but it seemed to be all they stocked.

Her cosmetics in hand, she tore through the clothes rack and within seconds, found an adorable black halter top, printed with tiny palm trees. A good sign, she thought as she charged her purchase and raced to the ladies' room and made the necessary repairs, exchanging the new black top for the tailored navy blue shell she'd had on under her gray suit. The black halter went well with the straight gray linen skirt from the suit and gave her a much-needed boost.

Now she waited nervously, sipping her drink and gazing around for Matt's approach. She definitely felt as if she was waiting for a date…and kept reminding herself that was not the scenario here. It was dinner with a colleague while on a business trip. Nothing more should be read into the invitation. He'd said it himself. It was just nicer to have company at dinner than eating alone.

If you weren't so attracted to him, you wouldn't have thought twice about the invitation, a little voice reminded her. You certainly wouldn't have run around like a ninny and bought a new top for the occasion.

True...but it's hard to think of Matt as unattractive. It's actually...impossible. Especially after watching him swim this morning.

The recollection brought another secret smile and the usual wave of embarrassment.

God, I hope he doesn't decide to bring that up....

She felt someone tap her shoulder and spun around, almost tipping her cocktail.

"Stephanie?"

It was only Ben. Stephanie instantly relaxed and took a breath.

"Oh...hi, Ben." He'd noticed that she'd changed and put on makeup. She could tell from his expression. She was relieved when he didn't comment. She felt self-conscious to have primped so much.

I hope Ben doesn't get the wrong impression.

Which would be...? That you have a crush on your boss? Seems that's pretty much the situation, Stephanie, another voice answered.

I do not!

Do too.

Do not!

You *so* do have a crush on him, Stephanie...and no backsies!

Ben was talking to her, she realized, but she'd missed half of what he'd been saying.

"I'm sorry…. What did you just say?"

"Matt said he's sorry but he can't meet you for dinner. He's tied up again. A few last-minute details to work out with the attorneys. He said to go ahead and eat. He didn't want you to wait any longer for him."

Stephanie felt her stomach drop. As if she'd been in an elevator that had missed a few floors. Now her new top and Provocative Pink lipstick felt very foolish. She shrugged, valiantly trying to hide her disappointment.

"No problem. I'm feeling pretty beat. I think I'll just head back to my room."

She slid down from her stool and grabbed her purse and jacket. Ben gave her a sympathetic look, which made her feel even worse.

For goodness' sake. Get a grip, she coached herself. It wasn't a date or anything like that. So you should hardly feel so stood up.

Nonetheless…she knew that she honestly did.

"Well, you really ought to eat something. I don't think I saw you have a bite all day. What if I fix you a tray and have somebody bring it to your room? You can be the only guest in the entire resort who gets room service tonight. How's that?"

Stephanie smiled. "That sounds great. If you find anything chocolate for dessert, send an extra big slice."

"No problem. I'll take care of it personally." He met her gaze. "Besides, I owe you one. You really saved my hide today."

His honest thanks was gratifying. Stephanie reached over and patted Ben's arm. "It's okay. I'm glad it's all worked out. In a few hours, it will all just seem like a bad dream."

Ben's expression grew more serious. "If Matt doesn't fire me, you mean."

Stephanie wasn't sure what to say. Ben was fishing, wondering if she knew anything. She couldn't blame him.

"I honestly don't know what he intends to do, Ben. He hasn't discussed it with me. I'll put in a good word for you, though."

Ben nodded. "Thanks, I'd appreciate that. I don't even need to stay on as general manager. Maybe I wasn't really ready for that jump. I realized today I was pretty happy down in food and beverage."

"Yes, I noticed that," Stephanie admitted. "You were positively masterful. I was wondering if you'd like to transfer back to that department. Would that be awkward for you?"

"Maybe a little at first. But I do love the work. Frankly, awkward is not the question. I have a family, kids, a mortgage. My wife is expecting another baby. I'm willing to do what I have to do. I just don't want to be out of a job."

He seemed so sincere. Stephanie's heart went out to him. "I can't promise you anything. But I'll talk to Matt about it."

"Thanks, I appreciate it." Ben nodded and smiled at her. "I'm going to work on your dinner now. I'll send it right over."

Stephanie thanked him again and headed off in the opposite direction, toward her room. She followed a path through high-arching palms that bordered the beachfront. The sand looked silvery white and the gently lapping waves, dark turquoise blue. A half moon hung over the bay, casting a shimmering beam over the bay.

It was a perfect night…for couples, Stephanie thought. She spotted quite a few walking on the shoreline, holding hands or with their arms around each other. She'd been noticing them all day. As busy as she'd been, she couldn't help but notice the honeymooners, the longtime married couples, the romancing lovers. The resort was positively overrun with them.

The place was marketed as a romantic getaway. What did she expect?

Still, she found it downright annoying at times. More than a bit depressing, too. It kept reminding her that she didn't have anyone in her life right now. No one to walk with or hold her hand. Or even eat dinner with.

No one to be her date at her sister's wedding, coming up only a few weeks from now.

Which made her think of Tommy Torelli. Was it right to break off their engagement? Was she expecting too much from life? From romance?

And where had this crazy crush on Matt come from? Stephanie was almost positive she hadn't felt this way back in New York. Maybe it was the palm trees and tropical flowers. The way he'd been looking at her while they worked down here. Or even something in the water.

Maybe it was feeling lonely and a reaction to breaking her engagement.

Stephanie let herself into her suite and flicked on a lamp. She kicked off her shoes and wriggled her toes. She felt tired but wound up. She'd been running at top speed all day and even gulping down a cocktail hadn't slowed her down much.

Out on the patio, the crystal water of the swimming pool beckoned. Maybe a few laps in the pool will help me unwind. Then a spell in the hot tub. That should get me tired enough to sleep.

One problem, no bathing suit.

Stephanie considered the challenge a moment and possible solutions. Matt hadn't let the lack of suit stop him this morning, had he, she mused. She'd never gone skinny-dipping, but something about the moonlight and her own restless mood seemed to be prodding her on.

Go ahead, Stephanie. No one's going to see you. You're such a goody-good. Be a little uninhibited for once in your life.

But what if Matt came back to his room early and peeked through his side of the fence, her sensible side countered?

So what? Your life might get a little interesting. Besides, you heard what Ben said. He's not coming back for hours. You're just chicken. You just don't know how to enjoy yourself.

No wonder you can't find an exciting romance.

Goaded on by her daring side, Stephanie decided to take the plunge and compromised with a swim in her underwear, a sensible pink cotton bra, edged with lace and matching bikini panties.

It practically looked like a bathing suit, she thought as she grabbed the terry-cloth robe and a towel. And no one was going to see her, besides.

She padded out to the patio, leaving the glass sliding door open so she could hear room service when her dinner came.

She dropped the robe and towel on a lounge chair and tested the water with her toe. It was perfect, like a tepid bath. She had no trouble slipping in and submerging up to her chin. She suddenly remembered her hair and quickly pulled out the pins, and dropped them on the pool edge. She dipped her head back and let her long hair fan out, floating behind her in the water.

Then she turned and launched herself to the far end, starting a lap with the breaststroke. The exercise felt good, even though she'd worked hard all day. The soothing water and steady rhythm of swimming worked out the kinks and knots, both mental and physical.

Stephanie did as many laps as she could, then climbed into the Jacuzzi, which adjoined the pool. She set the timer for twenty minutes, flipped on the switch and sat back as jets whipped the warm water into bubbling foam.

Swimming had been a good idea. She felt refreshed and relaxed, the anxieties of the day magically washed away. Even missing out on dinner with Matt didn't seem such a disappointment.

Just as well, Stephanie thought. He probably would have been charming and attentive, making me feel as if he was really interested, and that would have made things even worse. Why even get my hopes up?

She leaned back to stare at the stars. There seemed a million of them. She blinked and yawned, feeling perfectly content and cozy, the soothing hot water covering her like a cozy quilt.

I'd love to make a wish, she thought groggily. I just can't pick one out to wish on.

They're all so beautiful....

Chapter Five

"Stephanie? Are you all right? For Christmas' sake, you're lucky you didn't drown...."

Stephanie felt someone jog her shoulder. She snuggled down deeper under the covers and tried to roll over.

Then she felt water in her mouth and suddenly sat up, coughing. She was sitting in water. She was freezing cold. She looked up to find Matt, crouched down next to her looking awfully concerned...and at the same time, annoyingly amused.

"Thank God. I thought you'd passed out or something."

"I'm fine." She stared up at him and realized she had on nothing but her underwear, which was now transparent. She quickly scrunched down under the water, trying to hide herself.

Matt stepped over to the lounge chair and held out

her robe. "Here you go. You'd better come out there. You're getting goose bumps."

"I don't have goose bumps. I'm fine," she argued. The water had cooled considerably and she was actually shivering. Her nipples had hardened to taut peaks, poking against the flimsy material of her bra, making it even more a necessity to stay submerged.

"Just put the robe down somewhere. I'll get it myself. You can go now, Matt. Thanks…." She glanced at him for a moment, trying to sound assertive. But she could see he wasn't going to budge.

"I'm afraid you might fall asleep again in there. I'll just wait until you're out of the pool. Come on now. I have my eyes closed, see?"

He held out the robe to her, both eyes squeezed shut.

"I'm not peeking…much," he teased her.

He probably thought her modesty was extremely silly, she thought. She'd bet the women he dated weren't modest at all about their bodies.

Well, you're not one of his babes. You work for him, remember?

"Well…are you coming? I'm not going to stand here like this all night."

"Just a second." Stephanie slowly rose out of the water. Her head spun and her legs felt like jelly. She *had* been in the hot tub too long. She tried to take the robe from Matt, but he wouldn't let go and she had no choice but to slip her arms in while he held it. She twisted around, fitting her arms in the big sleeves, then grabbed for the belt as he finally let go.

He opened his eyes and looked at her. She gazed up at him and tried to smile. Then, yanking the belt into a knot, she felt herself blink and the entire scene blurred and spun.

Matt reached out and grabbed her just before she lost her balance and fell headlong into the tub again.

"Whoa...I've got you. Just hold on. It's okay."

With his strong arms wrapped around her waist, he led her a few steps away to a lounge chair and gently let her lie down. Stephanie felt the dizziness pass and took a deep breath. "I'm sorry. That was so dumb of me. I guess I did sit in there too long."

Matt sat on the edge of the chair, staring down with concern."Did you have anything to eat tonight?"

Stephanie had to think for a second. "Gee...I guess not. Ben was sending me a tray, but I never heard room service. I must have fallen asleep. How did you know I was in the pool?"

"I peeked through the wall," he admitted. He grinned. "So now we're even, right?"

She felt her cheeks get warm with color, but didn't answer. "What time is it?"

"Nearly one." He sighed and stared down at her. He reached out and whisked a few strands off from her cheek with his hand. She secretly thrilled to his touch, though he seemed hardly conscious that he was being so familiar with her.

"I'm sorry I missed our dinner. The attorneys got me tied up again and then I ended up waiting for the employees to go back on the job at midnight."

"Well, at least that's all settled. You must be relieved."

"I am." He nodded. "But I couldn't have gotten through this without you, Stephanie. You did a superb job today and I'm very thankful."

Stephanie felt awkward hearing all his praise. At such close range it was a little hard to take. He sat so close, staring down into her eyes.

"Oh, you would have managed all right. I'm sure you would have."

"I don't think so. You're the first person I thought of to help out down here. The only one, to be honest. I can see now my first instinct was right."

His confession made her pulse race and she tried hard to hide her reaction.

So he did think of her in a special way it seemed. He had noticed that she was more than a new piece of office equipment. Of course, the type of woman a man calls to help with a business emergency hardly signifies a wild, hot attraction, she reminded herself. Still, she felt honored by his compliment.

"Thanks, that's nice of you to say," she replied, feeling that she sounded sort of lame.

"I didn't say it to be nice," he replied, his expression an unreadable mask. "It's just the truth."

Now he had her. She found men hard enough to deal with under the usual circumstances. But when they started being truthful—watch out.

When she looked up into his eyes, Stephanie knew for sure it was time to say good-night and go inside.

But it was hard to go. He now sat turned towards her, his big body hovering over her. She stared up into his dark eyes, feeling mesmerized. She didn't know what would be worse, if he tried to put a move on her...or if he didn't.

His gaze swept over her, roaming over her face, her neck and breasts, exposed by the gaping robe. She shifted restlessly, her body tingling with awareness as his gaze moved lower, lingering on her smooth, bare legs. He reached over and pulled the edge of her robe over her knee, a tiny gesture that seemed outrageously intimate.

When she turned to him, she felt her breath catch in

her throat, her entire body tingling with awareness. He was standing so close, she breathed in the scent of his soap and his skin. Outlined in moonlight, he looked so powerful and masculine. So powerfully attractive to her.

She racked her mind for something flip and funny to say. Some quick, smooth exit line that would break the mood and ease her out of the door. But her mouth felt dry, the right words wouldn't come. When she met his deep blue gaze, she felt frozen to the spot, her pulse racing out of control.

His expression was serious, unreadable. And totally intense. He lifted his hand slowly and touched her hair. It had already started to dry and he let the thick, wavy locks fall against his open palm.

"You have such beautiful hair. I've never seen it down like this." His words were quiet, practically a whisper.

"I don't wear it down much…. It gets in the way."

He laughed lightly at her answer. "I'd imagine that the problem is more like *men* get in the way," he replied in a deep, husky voice as he moved even closer. "This one can't resist…."

Her impossibly handsome boss was about to kiss her. On a lounge chair. While she was less than half dressed and surrounded by tropical flowers and drenched in moonlight.

And she was going to let him.

Was this really happening to her?

She thought to pull away, but her body felt so warm and heavy, rooted to the spot. She stared up at him, studying the hard lines of his too-handsome face, his dark eyes, his square jaw and wide, soft mouth. His hand moved from her hair to cup her cheek and before

Stephanie could utter another a single word of protest, his mouth captured hers in a deep, savoringly sexy kiss.

His kiss was bold and hot. It was hungry and intense. A knockout sensual punch that sent Stephanie's senses spinning.

She knew it was wrong to kiss him back, to give in so easily. But all logic was totally short-circuited as Matt's mouth glided over hers, teasing and tasting, coaxing her full response. Her hands rose up to his hard shoulders, in a half-hearted attempt to push him away. But the feeling of his firm muscles under her fingertips instantly melted her last drops of resistance.

She made a small moan in the back of her throat, a sound half of pleasure…and half admission to her surrender.

It was more than enough encouragement for Matt and she swiftly felt his response, his embrace tightening as his tongue plunged into her mouth, sliding seductively against her own. He quickly stretched out beside her, his long hard body pressed close to hers. His large, strong hands glided under her robe, sweeping over her breasts and hips, then down to cup her bottom, pulling her close to his heat.

Despite all rational and moral objections that raced through some saner part of her mind, Stephanie was swept away by the moment, giving herself over to the wave of sensual pleasure that crashed down over her, like a tidal wave.

Matt's lips left her mouth and wandered in a scintillating path down the column of her throat. She moaned as his warm mouth covered the tip of her breast, teasing her nipples through the thin wet fabric of her bra.

She moaned and twisted in his arms. "God, you're

beautiful," he sighed as his mouth met hers again. Their passions met in another deep, breathtaking kiss.

What was happening here? She wondered vaguely as she kissed him back. Tommy Torrelli had never once kissed her like this.

No one had ever kissed her like this.

Every doubt she had about Matt being attracted to her instantly vanished. This man was definitely attracted. Wildly attracted. Like a volcano about to explode.

And she felt the same. Never once had she felt this way in any man's arms. So vibrantly alive, so wild and uninhibited....

Totally amazed at her own reaction.

Matt pulled away, just far enough to look into her eyes.

Her robe was hanging loose around her body and their legs were entwined. She felt him, hard and ready, straining against his trousers.

He sighed, seeming breathless and stunned. "I want you so much. I want to just hold you and make love with you. All night long."

She felt dizzy again, her head spinning at his bold confession. He pulled her close and pressed his cheek to her hair. "Just tell me what you want, Stephanie. Whatever you say, it's all right. I'll understand."

Stephanie couldn't speak. She held him close, her hands wandering hungrily over the hard planes of his shoulders and back.

You can't make love to your boss! Not out here, on a lounge chair for goodness' sake!

Her goody-good, ever practical, nice-girl side was shocked. Get hold of yourself! Put your clothes on! Sure, he wants his fun. But what's going to happen tomorrow?

Stephanie considered the question.

I don't care, a bold little voice replied.

Her eyes flew open. I don't care, she realized. I just want this man. Right here, right now.

For once in my life, I'm going to do something wild and impulsive. I'm going to take my crayons and color outside the lines. I'm going to be…swept away.

Then she silenced all the little voices arguing in her head and took Matt's face in her hands and pulled him around so that they were facing each other again. She gazed long and deep into his eyes, seeing that he was just as in awe of this amazing connection they seemed to have with one another as she was.

"I want you, too," she said quietly. She moved her head closer and kissed him. "Let's just…."

She never got the chance to finish her sentence. Matt swiftly pressed his mouth to hers again, his kiss all-consuming. His hands moved to her shoulders, smoothing the thick robe off her body and tossing it to one side. He quickly pulled off her bra, covering her shoulders and breasts with soft warm kisses and stroking her nipples with his fingertips.

Matt's shirt was already half unbuttoned and his tie undone, but she could hardly keep her mind on the task of unfastening the rest of the buttons and removing it entirely.

She felt the heat building in her body and arched herself against him. His hand moved from her breasts to her flat belly and then down over her womanhood. He slipped his hand in her panties and stroked and teased her with his fingertips until she could hardly stand it. Her pleasure was so intense, she writhed against him and heard herself helplessly moan. He pulled her panties off her legs and touched her even more freely. He seemed to know just how and where to touch her, anticipating her needs so perfectly, he seemed to be reading her mind.

She pressed her cheek to his hard chest, feeling the crisp hair against her skin. She licked and teased one flat masculine nipple, pleased at his reaction.

With her hands on his hips, she undid his pants and moved them down over his long legs. Matt quickly took care of the rest, tossing his pants and shirt in a heap with the rest of their clothes.

Stephanie moved her hands slowly over his body, stroking his stomach and legs. She sat up and dragged her long hair over his skin, kissing a path over his chest and hard flat stomach. She felt his hardened manhood in her hand and stroked him gently. His groan of satisfaction excited her and she felt a strange power over him. One she'd never expected.

"God...I love the way you touch me, Stephanie. You're so sexy...I can't believe it...."

Stephanie could hardly believe it either. Something about Matt, about this night, had turned her into a siren. As if she'd drunk a magic potion and had fallen under a spell. Maybe tomorrow she'd turn back into her same old, sane little self.

But tonight, in Matt's arms, she felt like a bold seductress and relished every minute of it.

Matt moved over her, and she shifted, wrapping her legs around his slim hips. Then he entered her and she felt her breath catch in her throat.

He stayed very still for a moment, hardly breathing. "God, you feel so good. I'm going to burst apart at the seams."

His husky whisper tickled her ear and she felt a small smile turn up the corners of her lips. He gazed into her eyes and she felt him starting to move, rocking his body inside of her.

"Did I ever tell you that you look like Mona Lisa? That sexy little smile you have sometimes? It really gets to me. It drives me wild."

Stephanie couldn't answer. She arched her head back, taking him even deeper inside. She could hardly believe the pleasure, pouring into every part of her body, as if all the hot white stars above were suddenly inside of her.

Finally, she was able to answer. "No…you never told me…. But now you know why she's smiling."

Matt laughed, his head dropping toward her. He kissed her deeply. "Now I know a lot of things I didn't know before, Stephanie. Or maybe I was just too blind to see…."

Then there were no more words for a long time as he began to move inside of her. Stephanie met him, matching his rhythm, feeling the heat building and building. Taking her higher and higher. Until she felt as if she was out among the stars.

They exploded together, falling headlong through the sky, leaving a long fiery trail.

Finally they lay quietly, their arms and legs wrapped around each other, Stephanie's head nestled under Matt's chin, pressed to his warm chest. He kissed her hair and gently stroked her back. Then he reached down, scooped up her robe and spread it out over them.

"Feel cold?" he whispered.

She shook her head, her eyes closed. "I feel perfect. Absolutely. Like I'm floating on a cloud."

"Me, too," he whispered. He stroked her hair and

pulled her even closer. She felt he wanted to say something more. She could almost feel the words welling up in his throat.

But finally, he didn't say anything. Or if he did, she didn't hear him.

She'd already fallen into a deep, sweet sleep.

Stephanie woke slowly. A slim shaft of sunlight slipped between the crack in the curtains in her bedroom. It looked so bright outside, it must be late, she thought. She stretched and yawned, feeling a smile stretch from ear to ear. She felt so rested and relaxed, as if she'd slept for days. As if she'd had lovely sweet dreams all night long.

All night long...sleeping in Matt's arms. Then, waking up again, making love and sleeping...and waking up, and....

Stephanie sat bolt upright, then yanked up the sheet to cover her bare breasts.

Oh my God! What did I do?

Her silent scream would have shattered glass. Her mental slap would have knocked her out cold.

Oh, what did I do? What did I do? What did I do?

I slept with my boss! Stupid, stupid. Totally... asinine.

Rule number one in the Smart Women's Handbook to Being Taken Seriously. Do not sleep with your boss. Do not tear his clothes off on a moonlit patio and make passionate love to him on a lounge chair.

You have a Masters in business administration. You would think you could have remembered that.

She stared around the room. No sign of Matt. The

other side of the bed was empty, though definitely disheveled. There were none of his clothes around and no sounds coming from the bathroom.

She sighed, first feeling relieved. Then feeling a letdown. Had he snuck out without saying a word? She guessed how he felt, shocked, embarrassed, mortified beyond belief.

But he could have said...something.

He could have at least left a note.

How would she ever be able to face him again? He must think I'm such a pushover. I didn't put up much of a struggle, did I?

I'll have to quit, that's the only solution. Maybe I can arrange a transfer. I wonder if there are any Harding hotels...on Mars.

She checked the time. Half past ten. She guessed that sooner or later Matt would be in touch this morning, at the very least, to tell her when they were leaving for New York. Maybe even to say he was sorry for taking advantage of her and it wouldn't happen again.

She cringed. She would hate that conversation. She couldn't let him find her like this, she decided. She had to clean herself up. Get back under control.

Stephanie dragged herself into the bathroom and turned on the shower full blast. She stepped in and soaped herself from head to toe. Wrapped in a towel, she raced around the suite, collecting her clothes from the most surprising places. Her underwear was still out on the patio, her bra and panties stuck in a flowering shrub. Luckily, the garments were dry enough to put on.

Back in the bedroom, she put on her suit, panty hose and heels. She swirled up her hair in its usual low twist and stuck in the pins with a vengeance.

She stared at herself a minute in the steamy bathroom mirror. Had he really told her she was beautiful? That she looked like Mona Lisa? She sighed. It seemed like a dream now.

She heard a sharp knock on the door and braced herself. It's showtime. She took a deep breath and fixed her face in a calm, bland expression.

She pulled open the door and Matt was standing there. Only he didn't look anxious and awkward as she expected. He certainly didn't look full of regret. He looked relaxed and happy, beaming at her in a most familiar way.

Then, his gaze swept over her outfit and he looked totally perplexed. "Going somewhere?"

She stepped aside and opened the door all the way. "I had a shower and got dressed."

"I think I like you better wearing a Jacuzzi." He grinned at her playfully and she blushed at the memory.

"Comfortable...but not very practical."

"Come on, Stephanie. You can't fool me anymore. I know that under that tailored gray suit, there's a sexy siren, just waiting to lure a poor guy like me to the rocks." He stared down at her and smiled affectionately. "And...how gladly I would go. Yet again."

He leaned over and kissed her. Just a quick sweet kiss on the lips. But the small gesture said so much. She stared at him. She couldn't quite believe it. But he seemed so...sincere. He wasn't acting distant and awkward, trying to deny or excuse their night together.

So that's where he'd disappeared to. He'd gone next door to shower and dress and call room service. She'd freaked out over nothing.

He actually seemed happy to see her.

"Feel like some breakfast?"

"Um…sure." She was in fact starved, having skipped dinner last night. Not to mention all the calorie-burning activity since then.

"Good. So am I. I'm ravenous." He glanced at her, and they both knew why. "I called room service. Everything's ready. Just follow me."

Tugging on her hand, he led her toward the patio.

They rounded the vine-covered partition and emerged on Matt's side, where Stephanie saw an umbrella-shaded table set with fine china, linen napkins and flowers. A serving cart stood nearby with a silver coffee service and several domed covered platters. Matt politely pulled out her chair and she sat down. Enticing smells filled the air and Stephanie took a deep appetizing breath.

"Hmm…something smells good."

"I didn't know what you like for breakfast so I ordered a little bit of everything. Give me your dish and tell me what you like."

Matt uncovered the various platters and served the food with all the grace and dash of a headwaiter. There was bacon, scrambled eggs, French toast, crepes and fresh pineapple and strawberries. Stephanie felt as though she could eat a house and asked for some of each.

It felt odd to have Matt serving her, more of that dream-like feeling she'd had last night when they'd made love. She realized she could have enjoyed it…if it didn't make her so nervous.

He served himself, poured their coffee and then joined her at the table. They didn't speak for a few moments, both enjoying their breakfasts and the wonderful quiet that surrounded them. The clear blue sky and brilliant sunshine promised another beautiful day in paradise, Stephanie thought. She gazed at the beach with regret that she'd had no chance to swim or even walk on the shoreline. But this was after all, a business trip...sort of.

"I'm glad to see you're not one of those women who won't eat anything but tofu and spring water."

Stephanie smiled. "The Rossis don't believe in diets. They would probably storm my apartment and stage some sort of intervention."

Matt laughed. "Food is one of the great pleasures of life, don't you think? It's just self-cruelty to deny yourself."

Her mouth full of French toast, Stephanie nodded her agreement. His talk of life's great pleasures brought to mind another great pleasure. She wasn't denying herself much on this trip, was she?

She swallowed hard, then sat back and wiped her mouth with the edge of the crisp linen napkin. "So...when do we get back to New York?"

Matt glanced at her. "In a hurry to return? I did promise to write you a note about Sunday dinner."

"Don't laugh. I might need it."

Stephanie nervously tucked a loose strand of her hair behind her ear. Matt reached over and helped her. She met his gaze and he cupped her cheek with his hand.

He seemed to know exactly what she was thinking. But he didn't say anything, just gently smiled.

"I was thinking, we could spend another day here. Relax, enjoy the island."

And each other, she knew he meant.

She stared at him and sighed. He was so unbelievably handsome. What woman in the world could resist? His dark eyes seemed to pin her in place, the edges of his wide, sexy mouth turning down into a coaxing smile.

She felt his hand cup her cheek, his fingertips tracing the delicate line of her jaw, a now familiar touch that had explored every inch of her. As impossible as it seemed, she wanted him all over again. If he tried to lead her back into the bedroom at that moment, she knew she would have followed.

Suddenly, the wave of dread she'd felt early returned. Full force. I can't do this, she realized with a sudden shock. I can't walk around all day in some fantasy bubble, knowing that sooner or later, it's going to pop.

Matt met her gaze with a questioning look.

"You don't want to stay longer?"

Stephanie shook her head. "I want to…but I can't."

He tilted his head to one side, looking puzzled. His hand slipped from her cheek and she felt the loss of his touch.

"You have some…obligation back in New York?"

She took a deep breath. "No, that's not it. I just can't do this. I know it's hard to understand. Last night was…wonderful. It was like a dream, really. But I don't want to have an affair with you, Matt. I don't want to have an affair with my boss. That's just not right."

She sat back and stared down at her hands. He sat back, too. When she looked up, he seemed surprised, but quickly composed himself.

"I see." He sat back in his chair and looked at her. "I understand. I didn't mean to take advantage of our relationship. I mean, the feelings seemed to be very mutual last night...."

"I don't have any regrets about last night. It was perfect and I mean that...."

"But you believe what you've read about me in the gossip columns, that I'm a womanizer and...what do they call it now? Oh, yes, 'a real player.' And you don't want to play? You're not that type, right?"

Stephanie didn't answer at first. She was sure those stories were exaggerated, though not without some kernel of truth. His reputation as a womanizer wasn't the real reason she didn't want to get involved with him. But it was certainly part of it.

"I wasn't expecting a proposal of marriage this morning, if that's what you mean."

"Don't think it didn't cross my mind." He flashed a mysterious smile and for a heartbeat, Stephanie had to wonder if he was teasing her or not.

"You might find this hard to believe, Stephanie, but I have an ironclad rule to never, ever get involved with my employees."

She did find it hard to believe. She was sure she wasn't the first woman who'd fallen so willingly into his arms. And she was even surer she wouldn't be the last.

"I broke my rule for you, Stephanie...and I agree, it was wonderful between us." He sighed and stared at her a long moment before saying more.

Was he waiting for her to say something? To change her mind and reconsider?

"I guess you're right. Maybe we should just leave it at that and forget last night ever happened. It's all my fault. I'm sorry. I should have been more responsible. I should have acted with more…self-control."

Stephanie felt stung by his apology. As if it had been a simple matter of self-control, keeping his hand out of the cookie jar. She'd felt it was more, much more. A power that had brought them together she never really thought existed outside the movies or romantic novels.

Now he had reduced it to a simple seduction scene, breaking his "rule" about fooling around with women who worked for him. A regrettable misstep that they could erase with a mutual attack of amnesia.

She laid her napkin on the side of the table and came to her feet.

"Maybe you can pretend this never happened. But I can't. I don't just fall into bed with a different man every day of the week, Matt."

"Of course you don't behave that way. I'm sure it's just the opposite. That's exactly why this wouldn't work. You're a wonderful woman, in every possible way…."

Stephanie held up her hand. "That's okay. Save the compliments for my letter of recommendation."

"What do you mean?" His eyes narrowed. "You can't quit on me, Stephanie…I need you. I need you to stay until Jerry Fields comes back. You know that."

"I'm sorry. I just don't think I can be your assistant anymore. I can't just forget this ever happened, Matt, and I won't be comfortable working so closely with you anymore. I'm sure you can understand that."

I can't just work with you, side by side, every day and remember how it was between us. How I felt in your arms. Have a heart, can't you understand that? she wanted to scream at him.

But their night together obviously hadn't meant

much to him, she realized, if he could carry on with business as usual so easily.

That hurt, too.

He stood up and faced her squarely. "You can't just walk out, it's totally...unprofessional. Besides, I was going to offer you a job in the head office. That would be a big jump for you. Do you really want to just toss away that opportunity?"

"I wasn't trying to get ahead by jumping on a bed, Matt. I think I can succeed without going that route, thank you."

Did he think for even one minute she'd gone to bed with him to help her career?! Now she was really angry!

He stared at her, then sighed with exasperation and ran his hands through his hair.

"Of course not. I never meant to say you did."

She looked at him and then away, folding her arms over her chest, mulling over all the possible replies she might deliver to him. The conversation was difficult enough. She didn't want it to end up in a screaming match.

"Can't we discuss this rationally? Like adults? You're twisting everything I say! I've never seen this side of you, Stephanie. It's...a shock to me."

Hell hath no fury like a woman scorned...and then bribed on top of it, she thought.

Besides, she thought she'd been mature enough this morning, resisting any further involvement with him, a day of fun in the sun. Another night of ecstasy between the sheets. Cruelly depriving herself of one of life's great pleasures, as he'd already pointed out.

For goodness' sake, how mature and self-disciplined did he expect her to be?

"Okay, I have an idea. Two weeks. You stay two

more weeks and train your replacement. I think that's fair enough."

Stephanie felt backed into a corner. But still, not ready to give in. She had willingly slept with him—very willingly—and knew she had to take some responsibility for this mess. Two weeks wasn't all that long. But considering the situation, it seemed like an eternity.

"What's the matter, don't you think you can resist me?"

He met her gaze, his tone low and teasing.

"Don't flatter yourself."

He smiled at her, waiting. "Two weeks and you can go back to your old job in operations."

"How about a transfer to some other hotel? Something outside of New York?"

His eyes widened with surprise. "If that's what you'd prefer I'm sure it could be arranged. What about your family? They probably wouldn't like you moving away."

"That would be my problem, wouldn't it?" Her eyes flashed at him. She turned and walked back toward her own suite. "Since everything is settled here, I'd like to return to New York right away. I can make my own arrangements if you need to stay."

She stood by the partition that separated the two patios. She watched as he considered her words.

"I think I will stay. I want to make sure everything gets back to order and I need to meet with Drury again before I go."

Stephanie suddenly remembered her talk with Ben the night before. How he'd asked her to put in a good word for him with Matt. It seemed an odd moment to discuss Ben's future, but Stephanie knew she'd most likely not have another chance.

"Are you going to fire him?" she asked bluntly.

Matt's expression showed no reaction. "I was on Friday night when we got here. Now I'm not so sure. He has screwed up incredibly though. How can I trust him?"

She could see Matt's hot emotions getting the best of his judgement. She hadn't known him long, but she already knew him well, she realized.

"I have a suggestion. I know Ben will agree to it, too."

She explained her idea of putting Ben back in the food and beverage area, as the chief executive there and bringing in a new general manager from another property. One who had more experience.

"He told me himself he thinks now he was promoted too soon. He'd be happy back in food service. He had a real talent for it, too."

Matt nodded, his gaze thoughtful. "That's a good solution, Stephanie. I should have thought of it myself. You see why I can't let you go?"

His tone was half joking and half serious, and his words cut her heart in two.

"In two weeks, you'll have to," she said quietly. "See you back in New York."

"Have a safe trip." He waved at her briefly, then dug both hands in the front pockets of his jeans.

Stephanie stared at him. For a moment, she wished everything could be different. She wished that they were running out to the beach together, hand in hand, the whole day and night ahead of them.

But that could never be, she reminded herself. Even if she wasn't his assistant, she still just wasn't his type. He'd said it himself; he was a player and she was more serious. Not at all the type to play.

Chapter Six

"You can pull up right here. That building with the flowerpots."

The yellow cab swooped over sharply and double-parked while Stephanie handed the driver a fistful of bills. She jumped out and had barely slammed the car door closed before the taxi sped away.

She felt relieved to be back in New York, where life was moving at warp speed. So fast, you didn't have time to think, much less sit around and sulk.

She stood on the sidewalk and stared up at her building, a narrow, four-story brownstone on West 86th Street, between Columbus and Amsterdam. Her apartment was tiny and dark, but her living room faced the street and she looked up now to see her window box, which she'd planted with bright pink geraniums and ivy.

She was good in a garden and had learned by helping her father with his annual patch of vegetables, tomatoes, zucchini, eggplants and herbs. Sometimes a stand of a sunflowers, too, which seemed incongruous in the middle of his city neighborhood. She'd love to have a big garden someday, but the window box and a few struggling houseplants had to satisfy her for now.

Stephanie had never been happier to unlock the building's front door, or climb the three long flights to her apartment.

Traveling back alone had been more than a good idea. A blessing, she decided. She would have lost her mind sitting next to Matt all those hours on a return flight.

She scooped up the pile of newspapers on her doorstep, twisted open the three locks and stepped inside. The place smelled a bit stuffy, though she'd hardly been away, and she quickly walked around, opening all the windows. Which didn't take very long at all.

It was a modest one-bedroom, even by New York standards.

There was an L-shaped living room and tiny kitchen that opened to the living room with a breakfast bar. Also a bathroom and bedroom about the square footage of the average elevator. When the rental agent had first showed her the place, Stephanie thought she might need to slant her mattress against the wall, and sleep on a diagonal. But the rent was so reasonable and apartments were so scarce, she was still eager to take it.

It wasn't much, but it was all hers, she liked to remind herself. Growing up, she'd always shared a bedroom with at least one of her sisters. Having a place of her own, that she could keep messy or neat, and decorate any way she pleased had been a real milestone.

After a quick shower she changed into sweatpants and a T-shirt. She heated a bowl of soup in the microwave and ate it with some crackers while leafing through the Sunday paper. Sunday always seemed to be the loneliest day if you were single. Today, of course, it felt even worse. But she didn't let herself linger on the reasons why.

Finally, she felt fortified enough to play back her answering machine. The number in the window showed eleven new messages and she was sure that ten at least would be from her family. She hit the button and sat back to listen.

"Stephanie, are you home yet, honey? Your grandmother said you went on a business trip, but she didn't know where. All she would tell us was a tropical island. That was a joke, right? I called your cell, but you never answered." A long pause. Stephanie thought it was over, but could still hear her mother breathing. "I guess you won't be back in time for dinner on Sunday. Too bad. I'm making your favorite, lasagna. Come by during the week and I'll give you some leftovers. Call me when you get in, honey? I just want to know you're okay...."

Stephanie knew her mother had called her cell phone at least twice over the weekend, but she hadn't had any time during the day to call back. And certainly no time last night, she recalled.

She thought about Matt for a moment, then forced his image out of her mind. How was she going to face him tomorrow at work?

She sighed. It couldn't be any harder than facing him this morning, she realized. Maybe the worst of it was over.

Two weeks. She'd be counting off the days, the hours, the minutes. She'd made the most colossally stupid mistake of her life and now she was paying for it.

Big time, as her dad would say.

She played the rest of the messages, her grandmother, each of her sisters, her youngest sister Angie twice, wondering if Stephanie had found a dress yet for the wedding.

Well, that was some benefit to her misadventure with Matt. It had been a total distraction from fretting about Angie's wedding. Stephanie was thankful that at least she didn't have to worry about being a bridesmaid again. She had stood up for her other sisters, but wasn't going to be part of Angie's bridal party. Though she loved her little sister dearly, she breathed a sigh of relief at the narrow escape.

It was all because of Jimmy Reilly, Angie's groom. He was uncomfortable with the elaborate wedding Angie had pushed for and had been dragged kicking and screaming into the plans. He drew the line at the size of wedding party and said he didn't want the photos of the ushers to look like a football team in tuxedos. A rookie officer with the NYPD, Jimmy worked out with weights, as did his pals. He had arm muscles the size of cantaloupes and a neck the width of Angie's waist. The football team photo was a distinct possibility.

Angie complained, but finally gave in and agreed to ask only three bridesmaids. She chose two close girl-friends and their sister Gina who was closest in age.

Their sister Christine was a bit miffed at being left out. A professional party planner, she loved to be center stage and share the spotlight—no matter how ridiculous the bridesmaid outfit.

But their sister Mary Ann, closest to Stephanie in age, was also relieved to be let off the hook. She was seven months pregnant and confided to Stephanie, "My prayers have been answered. I'd look like a satin-covered minivan in that gown Angie picked."

Stephanie knew she'd gladly trade places with Mary Ann, even if she did look like an SUV lately. I wish I was pregnant, she thought vaguely. That would put a lid on my gossiping relatives. Or at least give them all something else to chatter about.

She was always the bridesmaid, never the bride, as the cliché went. Even if guests didn't say it right out loud; whenever one of her sisters was married, she knew they were thinking it. It was bad enough she didn't have a date.

Hopefully, I can keep a low profile and just blend in with the wallpaper. It won't seem so obvious that I'm the only complete loser in the family.

As long as Nana doesn't push me up there to catch the darned bouquet.

Stephanie sighed. Her life seemed so bleak. Her apartment seemed so…empty. Maybe it was time to follow Aunt Lily's example and get a few cats.

The buzzer on the downstairs lobby rang. She jumped up, wondering who it could be.

Don't even think about it…Matt is probably still in Florida and he doesn't know where you live.

Still, she felt a bit breathless pressing the intercom. "Yes, who is it?"

"It's me, Tommy. I was just in the neighborhood. I thought I'd drop by and say hello."

Stephanie felt her jaw drop. She wasn't sure how long she stood there, considering the implications of this surprise visit from her ex-boyfriend.

"Stephanie? Did you hear me? You gonna buzz me up, or what?"

"Um, sure. Just a sec." Stephanie pressed the button and unlocked the front door for her visitor.

She ran into the bathroom and checked her reflection in the mirror. She looked about as wretched as she felt. Her face was bare of makeup, her eyes were puffy from crying on the plane and her nose was red. Her hair was still damp from her shower and hung in long straggly waves.

She pulled her hair back with a clip into a low ponytail and splashed some cold water on her cheeks. She considered lip gloss but couldn't find any in the medicine chest and when the front doorbell rang, she said to herself. "What the heck, it's just Tommy."

She ran barefoot to the front door and pulled it open. "Hi. Gee. What a surprise."

He nodded and walked in. "Hey, how you doing?" He looked her over. "Gee, Steph. Good to see you. You look…terrific."

Stephanie shook her head and nearly laughed at him. "Come on, Tommy. I've known you too long. I look horrible."

He shrugged, his wide shoulders shifting inside his leather jacket. "Not to me you don't. You never look **horrible to me, kid." He thrust out his hand and she** suddenly noticed he was carrying a bouquet of flowers. Just the quickie-kind you can pick up at the greengrocer on the corner. It's the thought that counts, Stephanie reminded herself.

"Here, for you. You look like you need a little cheering up. If you don't mind me saying so."

She glanced at him and took the flowers. "Thanks. I'll put these in some water."

He followed into the kitchen and sat at the small snack bar watching her. She found a glass vase and filled it with water, then unwrapped the flowers.

"So...what's up?"

"Oh...not much," she said lightly. "What's up with you?"

"Life is good." He nodded solemnly. "I got that promotion I was up for."

She turned and smiled at him. "Good for you. Congratulations."

He smiled proudly. "Thanks a lot. I'm in charge of a whole division now. It's a hefty raise, too. I've got a new office. No more cubicle. And an extra week's vacation." He dug into his back pocket and pulled out his wallet. "Here, you want to see my new card?"

"Uh...sure." She turned and took his business card. Tommy Torrelli, CPA. Division Manager.

"Nice. Very nice." She glanced at him and forced a smile.

Tommy was obsessed with the corporate pecking order. Stephanie liked her job and hoped to advance, but she didn't dwell so much on titles and office size, or all the other status symbols of the office food chain. It was a quirk of his that had eventually gotten under her skin and she was now acutely reminded of one reason she'd broken off their relationship.

"Yeah, they just told me on Friday. I haven't even celebrated yet." She carried the flowers out to the living room and set them on the coffee table. Tommy followed her.

"I was thinking, Steph, would you like to go out to dinner or something? To celebrate with me, I mean?"

She stood up and looked at him. She didn't know what to say.

He seemed so...vulnerable. She didn't want to hurt his feelings. They'd parted on mostly good terms, agreeing to be friends. But this didn't seem an entirely friendly invitation. She just had that feeling.

"Gee...Tommy. You caught me by surprise. I just got back from a business trip. I'm really beat. I don't think I'd be very good company tonight."

He shrugged. "I didn't mean tonight. I just meant, you know, sometime." He took a deep breath and tried to catch her eye.

"I've been thinking about you, Stephanie. I've been thinking about you a lot. I really miss us being together. Talking to you. Just hanging out. It wasn't all bad, was it?"

"Uh...no, of course not. It wasn't bad at all. I mean, we got along okay. Most of the time."

"Well...that's a lot, don't you think? I mean, it's a cold, cruel world out there. It's hard to find somebody you can get along with."

She sighed and clasped her hands together. Oh, gee. She had a feeling this was his real agenda. She had felt it in her bones the moment she'd heard his voice through the intercom. She wished that a hole in her well-worn area rug would open up and swallow her whole. She just didn't know how to handle this...what to say....

Why did he have to come tonight, of all nights?

"Tommy, I've had a long weekend, working. I'm sorry. I just don't feel up to having this conversation right now."

"What conversation? I was just...you know, talking. Talking in general." He sighed again and stared at her. "You know what I'm getting at, Steph. I want us to get back together. Couldn't we just try?" He took a step toward her. "We could just, you know, date. Nothing heavy. I won't put any pressure on you. We'll go out, have some fun. Like we used to do. Just see where it goes."

She glanced at him, then turned to look out the window. She could put this off. She could tell him she wasn't sure. She had to think about it. She could give him some convenient excuses then lead him to the door.

But that wouldn't be fair to him. It would give him false hope and in her heart she knew there was no chance she'd ever renew their relationship. Perhaps there had been some small chance even a few days ago, before she'd gone away with Matt. Maybe she did have some lingering doubts, some regrets that she'd acted too hastily. Tossed away a good thing.

But now there were none.

She felt like a woman who had walked on the moon, who knew what it looked like on the other side of the stars. She had long suspected that there was life beyond dinner, a movie and the predictable passions of Tommy Torrelli. Now she knew for sure. It was true. If she never experienced that height again, at least, for once in her life, she knew.

Just as surely, she knew that Tommy was not the one

and would never be. So it was wrong now to give him any reply but the truth.

She turned to him slowly and swallowed hard. She could tell from his expression that he'd already guessed her answer. "Tommy...I'm very touched that you came over to talk to me. I'm sure it wasn't easy. I think you're a great guy, a great person. Really. I always hope we can be friends...."

"But you don't want to see me. You don't want to get back together," he finished for her. "That's what you're trying to say, right?"

His tone was low and rough. He was hurt. But there was nothing she could do.

"I'm sorry. I just don't think it would work out."

She would have said more, but he tossed up his hands in a gesture of surrender.

"Okay, I got it. You don't have to say any more. I've got the picture." He turned and headed for the door, without even looking at her.

"Geez, it didn't take you very long, Stephanie, did it?"

"What?" She followed him a few steps, then stopped at the edge of the living room.

He pulled open the door and turned to her. "It's written all over your face. I know you from grade school, remember?"

"*What's* written all over my face?"

"You've met somebody new. I can tell. You can't fool me."

"I'm not seeing anybody, Tommy. That's not true...and that's definitely not why I won't go out with you anymore."

"Okay. Whatever." He shook his head, looking frustrated. "I don't know what you want out of life, Stephanie. But I hope you found it."

Not yet, she wanted to answer. Not by a long shot.

"I hope you find what you're looking for too, Tommy. Honestly."

"Thanks. Thanks a bunch." He stared at her a second, a cold angry look that chilled her heart. Then he whirled around and slammed the door.

Stephanie stood a moment in the middle of the living room, feeling stunned. She dropped into an armchair and closed her eyes.

What a day. What a day from—

The phone rang and she let the machine pick up. Bracing herself, she listened to the message coming through the speaker.

"Stephanie? It's Nana. Did you get back from the tropical island yet? I gave them the message, but they didn't believe me. What else is new? Your father thinks I'm losing my marbles. The way he talks to me lately. He's got no respect. By the way, Tommy Torrelli came around this afternoon. He had that look, like a sad hang dog." Stephanie knew that Nana meant hound dog, but she always mixed up the words.

"I think he's trying to get back together with you. You'd better keep your eye out...I lit a candle for you at church today. You call your Nana, okay?"

The beep sounded and Nana Bella hung up.

Stephanie slapped herself on the forehead. *Thanks for the warning, Nana. Only about twenty minutes too late...*

Stephanie sat in her office, sorting out memos and the weekend updates from various hotel departments.

Her stomach jumped at the least sound in the hallway outside. But she knew that Matt would probably not arrive at his office until nine, at least an hour from now. For all she knew he was still on Blue Cay and hadn't even returned yet to New York.

The way her luck was running lately, that easy break seemed unlikely.

She could have asked his secretary Margaret Waters, who sat just outside his door. But for some reason, she didn't want to.

She'd dressed carefully that morning in a navy blue suit with a high neck, long jacket and slim skirt. A suit she thought of as her body armor, a prison-matron look reserved for tough meetings and the occasional funeral. Her hair was pulled back in its usual prim style and the only jewelry she wore was a watch and a set of pearl earrings.

It was not exactly a "dress to impress" outfit...but more of a "dress to discourage" look. To discourage Matt from thinking that she had any lingering urge to jump into bed with him again.

It seemed unbelievable to her. They actually did have an affair...didn't they? Even though it was only one night—one wild, glorious, unforgettable night— it had happened.

Some might see it as a textbook case, the classic dilemma of a female executive, maneuvering through the minefield of a male-dominated, corporate environment. Stephanie knew it was something different altogether. The banana peel most women would have slipped on working for Matt Harding. There was something about him that just got to her, that made her lose all reason, all control. Temporary insanity, that was her plea. Looking at it that way, she'd finally decided not to be so hard on herself.

If anyone in the hotel ever finds out, I'd just shrivel up and die, she thought. Matt was a gentleman. He'd never talk about their one-nighter, she told herself. But what if Tommy had been right? What if people could just look at her and guess?

You're being ridiculous, Stephanie. Get a grip. She slipped a compact out of her purse and checked her reflection. She did look different. More like dreadful than filled with desire, though. The only thing anyone might suspect is really bad PMS. Or maybe a stomach virus.

She turned to her computer and checked Matt's schedule. He had a meeting with the finance department at nine-fifteen. One she didn't have to attend, thank goodness. She decided to avoid him by heading down to human resources and getting a quick jump on searching for her replacement.

The sooner she found someone to take her place, the sooner this nightmare would be over. She wasn't sure how he'd talked her into staying two more weeks and cursed her own weakness now for ever agreeing to it.

Two weeks. She opened her own appointment calendar and made a giant star on the day. She wasn't sure how, but somehow, she'd make it. After all, she was a Rossi and made of stern stuff.

With a final gulp of coffee, she tossed the empty paper cup in her trash basket and headed out the door.

You can do this, Stephanie. Whatever doesn't kill you makes you stronger...right?

Avoiding Matt was not nearly as difficult as Stephanie had anticipated. He returned late on Monday afternoon and she was hardly aware he was in the hotel until she was about to go home. Then, only by catching a glimpse of him through a crack in the door while he talked to his secretary.

After the second day, it dawned at her that he was trying to avoid facing her as well. Instead of bellowing into her intercom, "Stephanie? Are you in there? I need you…" at regular intervals, as he usually did, he now resorted to using e-mails, voice mail, or sending her memoranda with yellow Post-its attached.

On Wednesday, day three, he sent her word that he was going out of town, visiting properties in Connecticut and Boston. Stephanie knew that he would have normally expected her to come along on such a trip, but wasn't surprised that this time, he did not. She was at first relieved to realize he wanted little contact with her over the next weeks, but at the same time, she was also disappointed. And even hurt.

Obviously, their night together didn't mean much to him at all. She was just another conquest, another fling. Another notch on his bedpost. He clearly regretted the entire episode and felt uncomfortable seeing her. He would be relieved when she was out of his office and out of his sight, she reasoned. She didn't mean anything to him.

Friday afternoon at half past four, she started the countdown. One week down, one to go. At the stroke of five she planned to mark the day off on her calendar, grab her overnight bag and beat a hasty retreat to the subway. She'd be spending most of the weekend out in Brooklyn, at her parents' house. Her sister's wedding was only a week away and the family was in a frenzy.

At five to five, Stephanie added a dash of lipstick and

smoothed out her hair, her usual quick repair before leaving the building. Rain that had started earlier in the day beat steadily against her office window. No umbrella or raincoat, she realized. She hadn't expected it. She'd look like a drowned rat by the time she reached Brooklyn, but what did it matter? She was just going to see her family.

She straightened out her desk for the umpteenth time, making a list of priority tasks for the following week. Matt still hadn't answered any of her notes about interviewing a replacement, nor had he returned any of the resumés she'd sent him.

How did he expect her to get someone in here by the end of the next week if he didn't make time for the interviews? She'd really have to get after him on Monday, even if it meant a face-to-face confrontation.

A sharp knock on the half-opened door brought her to attention. She sat up sharply as Matt poked his head inside.

"Good, you're still here. Can I speak to you about something?" He walked in and stood in front of her desk.

"Of course. Is anything wrong?" She heard herself stammer and felt embarrassed. It was just a shock, seeing him there.

She hadn't seen him in nearly a week and the sight of him jolted her senses instantly awake. He looked very corporate and intimidating in a navy blue suit with a fine chalk pinstripe that accented his broad shoulders and long legs. An off-white shirt contrasted with his bronzed skin and a burgundy silk tie, loosened at the neck, complemented his dark eyes perfectly. His thick, slightly wavy hair was combed back straight from his smooth brow and along his strong, square jaw she spotted a hint of five-o'clock shadow.

He seemed so tall, dark and one hundred and ten percent male. She'd been berating herself for the past few days, wondering what had gotten into her down in Blue Water Cay.

Well…duh. Reality check. It wasn't so hard to figure that out.

He smiled slightly and sat down in an armchair in front of her desk. "Don't worry. I'm not about to announce an emergency excursion to a tropical island."

"I think I'd have to pass this time."

She saw his smile fade a bit. "Just as well then. I know I'd be wary of facing it without you."

He meant that as a compliment, she guessed. But it only made her feel worse about the way things had turned out between them.

"I know it's getting late. I don't mean to keep you." She saw him glance at her overnight bag, which sat in clear sight beside her desk. "You're probably eager to start the weekend."

"Well…yes," she admitted.

"I just wanted to pass on this report I got from finance. Could you take a look at it over the weekend? There are a few items that don't look right to me. I've made some notes."

Stephanie took the folder from him and laid it on her desk and flipped it open. It was hard seeing him again at close range, she decided. But the perfect moment to confront him about interviewing her possible replacements.

She took a few calming breaths to slow down her heartbeat, then recalled the advice from a book she'd read the night before. Unable to sleep, she'd gotten out of bed, looking for something to distract her. She'd found a self-help bestseller about relationships, *Snap Out of It! — A Smart Woman's Guide to Kicking Dumb Romance Habits*.

When she felt her resolve slipping, she was supposed to give herself a mental slap. When she had to face Matt, she was to imagine his face replaced by a cartoon character.

She glanced back up at him, dark eyes sparkling and his mouth holding just the hint of a smile. Who should he be, Daffy Duck? Scooby-Doo?

He bowed his head a moment, looking at his own copy. "You don't need to read it through right now. Unless you have some questions?"

He didn't remind her anything of a goofy dog. Or a stuttering duck. On his very worst day. His cheeks were too lean and his features too chiseled to ever resemble SpongeBob SquarePants or Homer Simpson.

This isn't going to work. I have to hit the mall this weekend and find a different book.

"I guess my handwriting is pretty awful. My father always said he thought I should be a doctor."

"Your handwriting is horrid," she agreed quietly. "But I'm used to it by now."

He looked up at her again. A lock of hair had fallen across his forehead and he smoothed it back with his hand. Stephanie remembered how it felt to run her hands through his thick hair, soft and springy to the touch.

"Sorry to ask you to work over the weekend. But it shouldn't take very long."

"It's fine, Matt. It's not a problem."

She scooped up the report and slipped it back in the

folder, then put the folder into her briefcase. He didn't have to drop in just to hand her a memo. He could have left it on her desk with a Post-it note. She waited, wondering why he'd really come.

He sat back and met her gaze. "I also want to speak to you about something else."

Something in his expression set off silent alarms. Her stomach rumbled with nerves.

"Sure. I have a minute."

He took a deep breath and sat back, his expression serious.

"It's about last weekend. You ran off so quickly, we never really had a chance to talk."

She swallowed hard. "Oh? I thought we did. I don't know that there's anything more to talk about, Matt."

"I think there is. I'm not sure you really understood what I was trying to say to you. Which was my fault entirely. I didn't express myself very…rationally after a while," he added. "You know how I lose my head sometimes."

"You? Never. The picture of patience. A regular Job." Her wide eyes belied her serious tone.

He laughed softly, a sound that nearly melted the rest of her best intentions. When she met his gaze his dark eyes were soft-looking, a rare moment he'd let his guard down. She'd hardly seen him this open and vulnerable-looking. Maybe in bed, she recalled, while they made love. The recollection made her defenses scatter. She looked away, feeling suddenly flustered. She didn't want him to know how much he still affected her.

She cleared her throat and sat up sharply. "We don't have to talk about this, Matt. In fact, I'd much rather we didn't."

"Oh…well, all right. If that's what you prefer." His brow wrinkled with a frown. "I just didn't want you to walk away thinking our time together wasn't…important to me. It *was* important. It was truly…wonderful. And I'm sorry if anything I said made you think otherwise."

Stephanie felt a lump the size of a golf ball lodge in her throat. Please stop, she begged him silently. I don't want to hear any of this. I know you mean well. But can't you see how much harder you're making it for me?

She took a deep breath. "I understand. You don't have to apologize. For anything. I think you were right when you said we ought to just forget it ever happened and move on." She picked up a file from her desk and handed it over to him. "I left this on your desk Monday. Maybe you didn't get a chance to look it over yet. I've collected some resumés of employees who I think would make good replacements for me. I thought it would save some time if you weeded them out. But I can set up interviews with all of them if you prefer."

He took the folder and sat back, his mouth set in a firm line, his face showing little reaction to her short speech. His gaze was closed again, she noticed. The warm, intimate light completely shuttered.

"I'd hoped that maybe you'd changed your mind about that."

Stephanie willed herself to stay strong. "No, I haven't. Not at all." She took a breath. "We made a deal, remember?"

"Yes." He nodded. "I remember. But I just wish you'd reconsider…."

He was so spoiled. A big spoiled baby! He had to

have everything his way! Didn't he think about her feelings for one measly minute? How hard it was for her to sit here and talk to him like this, even for five minutes?

She felt so angry at him all of a sudden, she thought if she didn't scream, she'd explode.

The phone rang, her direct line. The red light flashed insistently. "Excuse me, I'd better take this," she said curtly.

"By all means." He sat back in a relaxed pose, looking as if he was willing to wait as long as necessary to continue their conversation.

"Stephanie, it's your mother," her mother Francesca greeted her. As if by now she wouldn't recognize her voice.

"Hi, Mom. I'm in a meeting. Can I call you in a few minutes?"

"I'm sorry to bother you, honey, but we have an emergency here...."

"Oh...what's wrong?" Her mother would now ask her to get off at Court Street, instead of the stop closer to the house, so she could pick up some fresh mozzarella or some other gourmet ingredient desperately needed for tonight's meal.

"It's your grandmother. She's disappeared." Stephanie could tell her mother was upset but trying to keep her voice steady. "We called around the neighborhood for hours. I was wondering if maybe you've spoken to her today? Maybe she called you at work, said she was going someplace?"

"I haven't heard from her." She glanced at Matt and guessed that she must seem alarmed, because he was looking at her with an expression of concern.

"What's the matter?" he asked quietly. "Is there some emergency?"

"Wait a minute, Mom." She covered the phone with her hand and turned back to him. "It's my grandmother. My mother says she's disappeared. They don't know where she is and they're getting worried."

He gave her a serious look. "You need some privacy. I'll go." He got up from his chair and headed to the door. "If I can help you any way at all, just let me know, okay?"

She nodded quickly and watched him go, vaguely aware of her mother still talking to her on the phone. "—And then we called her other friend, Freda Spivek, but she hasn't seen her since Wednesday. Your father is beside himself. He even went down to the police station. He didn't even eat lunch...."

Stephanie took a breath. "Don't worry, Mom. I'm sure she's all right. She's probably shopping or visiting a friend and just forgot the time. I bet she's home in time for dinner."

"Oh, I hope so...the thing is, she and your father got into another one of their arguments. You know how she gets. She went up to her room and slammed the door. I went out shopping and when I came back, she was gone. She even took the big gray Samsonite with the wheels out of the attic." Her mother's voice quivered, on the verge of tears. "I should have never left her alone.... But I never thought she'd run away like that...."

"Mom, it's okay. It's not your fault," Stephanie soothed her.

It was worse than she'd thought. Nana had stormed out of the house in a huff plenty of times. But never with a suitcase.

"Maybe it's not my fault entirely, but your grandmother is out roaming around the city, God only knows where."

"She'll be fine, Mom. Honest. Try to calm down a little." Stephanie sighed. "I'm coming right over. I'll be there in less than an hour."

Stephanie wasn't sure what she could do to help find Nana Bella, but her parents definitely needed her support right now. She was sure that her entire family would be converging tonight on the little house on Sackett Street.

Stephanie hung up the phone and heaved a gigantic sigh. She looked up to find Matt standing in the doorway to her office. He was carrying his briefcase and looked as if he was leaving his office for the day. But he'd waited for her, she realized.

"Going out to Brooklyn?"

She nodded and picked up her duffel bag. "I'd planned to go there for the weekend anyway. There's a lot to do to get ready for my sister's wedding. But now with Nana gone, it's really going to be bedlam. A real Italian opera." She forced a smile but was actually quite worried about her grandmother.

"Can I help in any way?"

She smiled briefly at him, heading for the elevator. "I don't think so. But thanks."

It was kind of him to be so concerned, she thought. Okay, maybe he wasn't such a spoiled dog after all. Maybe he did have a thought for other people, once in a while.

She pushed the button for the elevator and stared at it, waiting, all the while painfully conscious of him standing close beside her.

"I'm driving out to Long Island tonight. To East Hampton. I can give you a lift."

Stephanie was unable to hide her surprise at his offer.

"You're going to drive me to Brooklyn?"

"Why not? It's right on the way."

Technically perhaps, Brooklyn was on the way to his beach house in the posh, legendary Hamptons. But in most other ways it was a galaxy away. More practically speaking, the Hamptons via Brooklyn was the route travelers most avoided. For one thing the Brooklyn-Queens Expressway had more potholes than the roads in Beirut and was perpetually under construction.

"Thanks...but I wouldn't want to put you out of your way."

"Don't be silly. It will be much faster than the subway and you'll never find a cab at this time of night. Especially with the rain."

It sounded as if he was traveling solo tonight, she realized. Did that mean he was dateless in the Hamptons this weekend? Maybe his date was meeting him out there. A weekend at the shore, made even cozier with the rain.

She shook her head, as much to refuse his offer as to clear out the unwanted images of Matt curled up in front of a fireplace with some other woman.

"Thanks. But it's okay. I'll just grab a cab out front."

"The line will be around the block. You'll wait forever."

She stared straight ahead, willing the elevator to arrive. "I'll be fine," she insisted.

The elevator pinged, the arrow pointing down. The doors opened and she walked in. He didn't follow, she noticed.

He stood at the doors, watching her before they closed.

"Thanks again, Matt. See you."

The doors closed on his simmering expression. He hadn't said goodbye, she noticed, just glowered at her.

The elevator reached the ground floor and she made her way to the front entrance. The lobby was bustling with guests, a typical Friday night. As Matt had predicted, the line for taxis was daunting, but she had no choice but to wait. She took her place, inching up every few minutes as a cab pulled up and picked up passengers.

She considered leaving the line and making her way to the subway, but the trains would be even more crowded than usual tonight with the wet weather and she might have to let one or more pass before she could wedge herself into the crowd.

It was a long ride to Carroll Gardens. Stephanie decided to treat herself to the cab ride, knowing she'd have enough stress tonight visiting her parents.

Nana had run off before. She'd always come back, unharmed. But never for such a long time. And never carting a suitcase. That was a new twist.

Maybe by the time she got home, there would be some news about her grandmother. Stephanie hoped so.

She looked up to notice that she was next in line. Rudy Phelps, the head doorman was handling the taxi line tonight. He smiled at her.

"Where you headed tonight, Ms. Rossi?"

"Brooklyn."

"You got it."

He jumped out into the street and waved a white gloved hand. He blew his whistle, an ear-splitting shriek. A yellow cab broke out of the flow of traffic and pulled up to the hotel's cab stand. Stephanie stepped forward but Rudy waved her back.

"Sorry, hon. That's not your car. You just wait up on the curb a second."

He waved on the next group up, a well-dressed couple who told him they were headed for the theater district. Rudy packed them into the cab, spoke briefly to the driver and they sped away.

Stephanie didn't quite understand why she'd been wait-listed, but these doormen and cabbies worked in mysterious ways. She sighed. A stream of water slid down her back and she shuddered.

She didn't notice the sleek black convertible pulling up to the cab stand until the car was parked right in front of her. Rudy jumped forward and pulled up the passenger side door.

"Here you go, Ms. Rossi." He smiled widely, and beckoned her forward.

She stepped toward the car, confused.

Chapter Seven

"Come on, Stephanie. Get in. You're getting the seat all wet." Matt leaned across the seat and called to her.

Rudy grinned and held the door open wider. "The boss wants to give you a lift. Of course, it's your decision entirely. But it sure beats the back seat of some broken-down old taxi."

Stephanie stared into the sports car's elegant interior and then at Matt's beckoning expression. Behind her, she could hear the others in line grumbling at the holdup.

She tossed her bags in the back seat. Then she slipped into the front seat and closed the door.

"That was a dirty trick." She pulled her seat belt down and clicked the buckle.

"Yes, it was." Matt rubbed the side of his cheek. Maybe to keep from laughing, she realized. "But all in the name of a good cause."

"I appreciate the gesture. But it isn't at all necessary. You can drop me at the next corner. I'll get the subway."

"No way. Next stop, Carroll Gardens." Matt glanced at her and grinned. "You can be very stubborn in your quiet way. Has anyone ever told you that?"

Many people had. But she didn't want to give him the satisfaction. "No, never." She delivered the bald-face lie with a slight shrug. She sat back, getting comfortable in her seat. The upholstery was buttery-soft leather, cream-colored. The sleek dashboard was polished wood with glowing dials and meters that looked more suited to the controls on a space shuttle. She had probably never been in a car this expensive in her entire life.

Rudy was right. It was like riding on a cloud. Infinitely more comfortable than bouncing around in the back of a typical cab.

But it was going to be a long ride to Brooklyn nonetheless. She felt so self-conscious sitting here, and darkly imagined opening the door and running out at the next red light.

Get a grip, Stephanie. He's just trying to do a good deed, to be friendly and helpful. Maybe he feels guilty about taking you to bed last weekend, she reasoned.

But thoughts of last weekend and their time together only made her feel worse. The car seemed so dark and close…such an intimate space. They were practically sitting shoulder to shoulder. He reached over and clicked on the radio, his face coming close to her own, the back of his hand brushed her knee. Strains of soft melodic jazz filled the silence.

Unsettled by the brief contact, Stephanie stared out her window as the city streets flashed by.

"Are you worried about your grandmother?" he asked after a while.

"A little. She's run away before. But she always comes back after a few hours. Or at least she calls and tells us where she's gone. My mother says Nana packed a bag this time. I don't think she's ever done that before."

"That does sound ominous. Why did she go, do you know?"

She glanced at him, wondering if he was really interested in this little domestic drama or just trying to be polite. She felt something in her heart flip over and she tried not to let her gaze linger on his face, the small attractive crinkles at the corners of his eyes, the long lines bracketing his wide mouth. He was too handsome for his own good. For her own good, more precisely.

Collecting her thoughts again, she said, "Nana Bella is my father's mother. About a year ago, he persuaded her to sell her house and come live with my folks. It seemed like a good idea at the time, but I don't think she's ever adjusted to losing her independence. She says my father treats her like she's already dead and buried...which isn't entirely an exaggeration." Stephanie added, considering her father's side, "He can be overprotective. But Nana can be very stubborn. She just doesn't know what's good for her sometimes."

Matt nodded, the corners of his mouth turning down in a grin. "That explains it then. I guess it's just genetic."

Look who's talking, she wanted to say. She'd never met a more single-minded man when he wanted his way. In and out of the bedroom.

"I'm sure she's okay and everyone is excited over

nothing. It doesn't take much to get my family going. They can be very dramatic."

"Yes, you mentioned that. But at least they care about each other. That's not the worst thing, you know."

He stared out at the road. Stephanie wondered about his expression. Was he thinking about his own family? She realized she didn't know much about his background, about any family ties. She'd never thought it appropriate to ask when they were working together and when things got more intimate, she'd never had the chance. He didn't have any pictures around his office, she'd noticed, and relatives never called. It was as if he didn't have any.

"What about your family, Matt? Do they live near here?"

He shook his head, staring straight out at the road. "My father lives in Palm Springs, California. With wife number four…or could be five. I think I missed number four altogether…. We've never been very close." His flat, unemotional tone was edged with quiet anger, she thought. "I have a younger brother, Greg," he added in a warmer tone. "He's an investment banker, quite successful. He lives in London. Has two kids and a great wife. We talk on the phone a lot, but I don't get to see them much."

The family scene sounded rather bleak. Or maybe she simply sensed from his careful words and closed tone that it was so.

Stephanie couldn't imagine being that distant from her family, physically or emotionally. What did he do for holidays? For birthdays? Of course he had friends, but it sounded so lonely to her, nonetheless. She wondered if his life had always been that way.

"Where did you grow up?"

"In Connecticut, mainly. We lived in Westport until I was about seven or eight," he noted, naming one of the wealthiest areas in the state. "When my mother died, my father sold that house and we moved to Greenwich. It was closer to his law firm in the city. Though we still didn't see him all that much."

Stephanie swallowed hard, realizing he'd lost his mother when he was only about seven years old. "That's sad about your mother," she said honestly. "That must have been hard for you."

He didn't answer for a moment, slowing the car to merge with the traffic entering the Brooklyn Bridge. "Yes, it was sad. It was very confusing for me and my brother. We just didn't understand what was happening when my mother got sick. But you learn to get past these things and keep going. That's what my father taught us to do. Everyone has setbacks in life. You can't dwell on the low points and let them hold you back."

Stephanie considered his reply, which sounded like a mantra from some self-help book. A pragmatic approach but one that seemed to deny deeper feelings. Was that what his father had taught him, how to deny his feelings? Or had this early, devastating loss simply taught him to protect himself from getting too close.

She could see that Matt had taken the lesson to heart and hadn't let the tragedy hold him back from being a great business success. But she sensed in some other, more essential way, he'd never gotten past it. Was that why he bounced from one woman to the next? Because he was afraid to love and lose?

Stephanie sighed and stared out the window again. It wasn't her place to psychoanalyze Matt Harding.

Even one night together—albeit a glorious one—didn't give her the right. She had no reason to sit here, sorting out his emotional baggage. They had no relationship but boss and employee and a week from now, even that tenuous tie would be cut.

As the car glided over the bridge, Matt turned to her and smiled. "This is my favorite bridge and one of my favorite views. The city looks beautiful at night in the rain."

The view of Lower Manhattan from the Brooklyn Bridge was one of her favorites, too. She'd often come to the bridge just to walk across on a sunny day. The skyline did look beautiful tonight, despite the wet weather.

Once they were over the bridge, Stephanie directed Matt through the backstreets of Brooklyn Heights and down Henry Street, toward her parents' neighborhood, Carroll Gardens. The streets were crowded with people rushing home from work, bringing children home from day care, shopping in the many stores or gathering in restaurants.

The winding streets were lined with well-kept brownstone and limestone buildings, many dating back to the 1800s. The neighborhood had warmth, charm and character. Which suited her family, Stephanie thought, since they *were* a bunch of characters.

As much as she loved having her own place in Manhattan, she always loved coming back here. The familiarity and comfort that seemed to surround her, like a cozy old sweater. Her family could drive her crazy at times. No argument there. But for Stephanie, there truly was no place like home.

"This is the street. Sackett. Just make a right. It's number 332," she told Matt, pointing out the house.

Matt pulled into a parking spot in front of the house and turned off the car. She turned to him. "Well…here we are. Thanks for the lift."

"No problem." He smiled at her, holding her gaze in the darkness. His face was so close, just inches away. She could see the golden lights in his dark eyes, which she'd only noticed the night they'd made love.

The recollection was a sobering one. She took a breath and quickly turned to open her door. "Thanks again. Have a good weekend—"

She was fast, but Matt was faster. He reached over the seat and grabbed for her bags, scooping them up before she could. "I'll help you with your stuff."

She stood on the sidewalk and waited as he walked around the car to meet her. "Thanks. I can take it from here."

He sidestepped her attempt to grab the bag and glanced toward the house. The door at the top of the short flight of steps was open, the yellow light framing her father and mother who stood waiting. Stephanie could only imagine their curious expressions after seeing her step out of such an elegant car.

"You don't want your family to think I have bad manners, do you? Not walking you to the door and introducing myself?" His tone was hushed, his expression definitely amused.

The fact that he was behaving like a man on a date with her was a bit unnerving. But after all her talk, he was probably just curious and wanted a glimpse of the infamous Rossi clan in action.

Stephanie knew when she was beat. "You probably lost points already for not dropping your cloak across that puddle. But looks like they want to meet you, too."

Stephanie climbed up the steps to the front door with Matt close behind. She briefly greeted her mother and father with a kiss on the cheek, then stepped back to introduce Matt.

"Mom, Dad…this is my boss, Matt Harding. He was on his way out to Long Island so he gave me a lift."

Matt beamed at them, holding out his hand toward her mother first. "Mrs. Rossi, how nice to meet you."

"Yes…nice to meet you, Mr. Harding." Her mother stood wide-eyed, staring up at Matt as if meeting a movie star. Stephanie fought off a deep impulse to cringe with embarrassment.

"Stephanie's told us so much about you…."

I did not! I never said a word! She glared at her mother, transmitting the silent, universal signal to shut up.

Luckily, Matt was busy shaking her dad's hand at that point and didn't notice. Dominic Rossi was known for a powerful handshake and for a moment, the two men seemed to be wrestling on the doorstep.

"Good to meet you. Thanks for giving Stephie a lift. Those subways are murder on a Friday night," her father rambled. "Why don't you come in, Mr. Harding? Get in out of the rain for a while."

"Yes, come in. Please," her mother urged him. "Take a little break from driving. The traffic must be terrible."

"Not so bad once we got over the bridge," Matt replied. Stephanie sensed he was about to accept the invitation and quickly jumped into the conversation.

"Matt has to run. He's got a long ride ahead of him. All the way out to East Hampton." She shot Matt a look. "I know you must be in a hurry to…to meet those friends for dinner."

She nodded at him encouragingly, holding his

puzzled gaze. I'm letting you off the hook, she silently telegraphed. Run. Now. While you still have a chance.

She saw a light of understanding flash in his eyes and he smiled at her. "You must have misunderstood me, Stephanie. I don't have any dinner plans tonight." He turned to her mother, flashing another megawatt, movie-star smile. "I'd love to come in and relax a few minutes, Mrs. Rossi…if it isn't any trouble. But I understand you're all very concerned right now about Stephanie's grandmother."

Smooth, she had to hand him that. His gentle decline sounded so much smoother than her hurried excuse.

"That's just the thing. We've had some good news," her father said.

"Did she call?" Stephanie pressed forward, eager to find out more.

"She didn't call yet. But we have a good idea where she's gone," her mother said.

"Come in the house and we'll tell you all about it. For crying out loud, why are we standing out here in the rain?" Her father reached out and rested his hand on Matt's shoulder, practically pulling him into the foyer.

Stephanie gritted her teeth as she shrugged off her damp blazer and hung it in the hall closet. Her father had already led Matt into the living room and had him seated in the La-Z-Boy recliner, the place of honor. Stephanie prayed he didn't turn it on to show off the heated seat and automatic back massager.

"How about a glass of wine, Mr. Harding?" her father was saying. "I have some nice Chianti here."

"That sounds great…by the way, call me Matt."

Stephanie turned to Matt with her back to her father

so he couldn't see. She shook her head. "No wine! Don't do it," she mouthed silently. When he didn't seem to get the message, she turned back to her father.

"I think Matt would prefer some bourbon, Dad. That's what you drink, isn't it Matt? Bourbon on the rocks…or maybe Scotch?"

Matt's mouth pulled to the side as he fought a smile.

"Chianti sounds perfect, Mr. Rossi. I'd love to try a glass."

"Sure thing. You call me Dominic and we're even."

Stephanie wilted onto the coach, directly across from her nemesis. Her father poured the wine. "Stephanie, honey, would you like some?"

"Sure, Dad. Why not?" Stephanie usually tried to avoid her father's Chianti. It gave her a headache and turned her teeth blue, even in small doses. But any port in a storm, she reasoned.

"So…what's the story with Nana? You still didn't say."

"It's been a day. Let me tell you. We called all her friends, all the neighbors. We even called the hospitals." Her father sighed and passed out the glasses of wine. "Your cousin Eddie, down at the police station, got all the patrol cars in the neighborhood looking for her. Meanwhile, about half an hour ago, we get a call from Maria Trento. Turns out your grandmother hopped a bus to Atlantic City. The Golden Age Club from St. Anthony's, they go every Friday. Maria's mother Rosalie called her from the bus on her cell phone, just to report in and happened to mention she was sitting right next to your grandmother. Maria knew we were frantic, so she called here right away to let us know."

"Well, that was a lucky break," Matt said.

Her father nodded. "She still didn't call, but at least we know where she is. What the heck. Let her kick up her heels a little, blow off some steam. The bus will bring her back on Sunday and we'll take it from there."

Stephanie worried at her father's tone. While he was obviously relieved to know that his mother was well and safe, he didn't seem to understand why she'd run off in the first place. Stephanie thought there would need to be some changes, especially from her father in the way he dealt with Nana Bella. But Stephanie didn't want to get into that conversation right now, especially with Matt hanging around.

"At least she's all right. I'm sure you're very relieved."

"You bet I am, honey. I don't think I've been that upset since your sister Mary Ann stuck that jelly bean up your nose. Remember that?"

The jelly bean story! Why in God's name did her father have to remember that mortifying episode, tonight of all times? She tried to keep a calm, controlled expression but it was a challenge, considering Matt's reaction.

"A jelly bean?" He burst out laughing. "I'm sorry...I never heard of such a thing."

"That's right. Kids will get into some mischief. We had to bring her to the emergency room. She was actually turning blue. And the crying. Mamma mia...." He shook his head dolefully.

"Dad...the wine?" Stephanie gently prodded her father to pass out the glasses he'd poured.

"Oh...sure. I'm sorry." Her father gave Matt a glass of wine and then gave one to Stephanie. He touched his glass to hers and then stepped over to Matt and did the same. "Salute. To your health," he translated for Matt's sake.

"Salute," Matt repeated, sans the Brooklyn accent.

Stephanie watched him sip the wine. His brows drew together sharply and for a moment, she thought he might spit the mouthful right out onto her mother's prized wall-to-wall carpeting. Then just as quickly, he forced a smile and swallowed it down.

Stephanie's father looked at him hopefully. "How do you like the wine, Matt?"

He didn't answer for a minute, looking knocked off balance by the question. "It's very…distinctive."

"I'll say. I make it myself. House of Rossi…" Dominic picked up the bottle and proudly displayed the label he had made at a local print shop. "That's the family crest. The Rossi coat of arms. Looked it up on the Internet."

He handed Matt the bottle. "Very nice," Matt said politely.

"I even grow some of the grapes out back. I make the wine down in the basement. One of my hobbies. Getting pretty good, if I must say."

"It has a very unusual…bouquet." Matt's diplomatic reply nearly caused Stephanie to burst out laughing. This was a man used to drinking the finest vintages in the world. Now he could add House of Rossi to his wine journal.

Matt glanced at a side table and caught sight of her mother's vast collection of framed photographs. The history of the Rossi girls, "from diapers to diaphragms," she and her sisters had secretly titled it. And everything in between. There were pictures in kiddie pools, on bikes, ponies, and water skis. Graduations and vacations. Birthdays and holidays. All the major sacraments, baptism, communion, confirmation and of course, proms and weddings. Except mine, Stephanie added in a silent footnote.

Matt picked up a photo, a slow smile spreading across his face. "Is that you, Stephanie? Your Sweet Sixteen?"

"Yes, it is." She snatched the photo away from him.

"My, my…weren't you cute," he teased her, his eyes quietly laughing. "I love the braces."

As Stephanie tried to frame some tart comeback, her mother bustled in with a tray of hors d'oeuvres.

"Oh, we couldn't get them off in time. But she was darling. A good girl, too. Never gave us a minute of worry."

"I can believe that," Matt said in a serious tone.

Stephanie just glared at him.

"Supper's almost ready," her mother announced. "We're just waiting for Angie and Jimmy. Then I'll throw on the pasta. Here's a little something to nibble on."

The familiar antipasto platter had been laid with extra care, Stephanie noticed. There were also small plates from her mother's best china, along with silver forks and linen napkins, all of which were usually reserved for holidays or visits from Father Vincent.

She set down the antipasto in front of Matt and he leaned forward eagerly. "Hmm, that looks good."

"Let me make you a nice dish." Her mother quickly heaped spoonfuls of olives, marinated artichokes and mushrooms, roasted red peppers, delicate curls of prosciutto, and chunks of provolone on Matt's dish.

"Wow," he said simply. He had already spread the

napkin on his lap and now took the plate with two hands. Stephanie's mother watched as Matt took a sampling taste.

"Delicious…" he mumbled soulfully with his mouthful. "The artichokes are sublime."

Her mother beamed. "I marinated them myself."

"Outstanding. I hope the recipe isn't a family secret?"

"We don't have many secrets around here. In case you didn't notice." Stephanie shot Matt a small tight smile.

"Don't be silly," her mother said. "Stephanie will tell you. Stephanie can cook, you know," her mother announced proudly. "She's a good cook, too. I taught her myself."

"I'm sure she is. She's an amazing woman."

Matt gazed at her with an indulgent smile. She felt her cheeks flush. Why was he so darned handsome? It just wasn't fair. Luckily her parents would chalk up the extra color to her father's home-brewed vino.

He speared a black olive with his fork, then popped it into his mouth and grinned at her. She suddenly wondered if he was doing this on purpose. Was he trying to get back at her for walking out on her job? He definitely could see that his hanging around was unnerving to her but he persisted in staying, just to get under her skin, she thought.

Her mother looked pleased at his appetite. "Help yourself to some more. Have some bread. It's from the bakery down the street. Delicious."

"Don't fill him up too much, Fran. He won't have any room for dinner."

"Dinner? Matt can't stay for dinner," Stephanie blurted out.

"He can't?" Her mother looked stricken. She turned from Stephanie to Matt. "Of course you can stay. We have plenty."

"Look at it out there, it's coming down in buckets," her father chimed in. "You'd be crazy to get on the road right now. You'll just be sitting on the Expressway. The Long Island Distressway is a better name for it, if you ask me." Her father grinned at his corny joke. Stephanie cringed. "Better to have a nice meal, here with us. By the time you're done, the rush hour will be over."

Stephanie felt the ball of knots in her stomach tighten. He *wasn't* going to stay for dinner...was he?

Please God...don't let him stay for dinner, she silently prayed.

Chapter Eight

Matt glanced at her and then back to her mother.

"Well…something does smell awfully good."

"It's just linguine with white clam sauce to start… and a little shrimp scampi for the entree. Oh, and some sautéed escarole. Nothing fancy," her mother said. "Do you like seafood?"

Stephanie glared at him but he carefully avoided making eye contact.

"I love it," he said sincerely.

"Then you got to stay. Fran makes the best clam sauce you ever tasted. Fresh clams, too. None of that canned stuff around here."

"Dominic, please. Don't be bragging about my cooking, you embarrass me."

"Embarrass you? What are you talking about?" Stephanie's father turned back to Matt, his expression doubly sincere. "My right hand to God. She's some cook…ask anybody. That's one thing a young man doesn't think about much when he gets married, but later…well, it matters, believe me."

Matt thoughtfully chewed a slice of pepperoni, nodding at her father's sage advice.

"So…you married, Matt?"

The pepperoni seemed to ball up in his throat and his eyes bugged out slightly. He swallowed hard.

"Uh, no…." He coughed, covering his mouth with the napkin. "Not at the present."

Her father looked shocked a minute by the answer, then suddenly laughed. "Not at the present time. That's a good one!" He laughed again and took another sip of wine. "I love it. Not at the present," he repeated again. "Me, I was born married," he confided with mock seriousness. "Fran and me raised five girls." He held out his wide, work-gnarled hand, spreading the fingers. "Five… Count 'em." He shook his head.

"They're all grown up now, and three down and two to go. Married, I mean. Angie, the baby, she'll be married next weekend," he added proudly. "That just leaves Stephanie. But her time will come," he added with a loving sigh. "She's the career girl. The fussy one."

"She's just waiting for the right man, that's all," her mother chimed in.

"Of course she is." Matt glanced at Stephanie. She couldn't meet his gaze. She didn't know if she wanted to scream…or cry.

Her father hadn't meant to mortify her. But everyone in her family tended to talk too much, especially once the bottle of Chianti came out. It didn't take long for a complete stranger to learn more than they ever wanted to know about the Rossis. All you had to do was sit in the living room and eat antipasto.

Stephanie sank deeper into the gold brocade couch, wishing the couch would just swallow her up whole.

"Stephanie, you set an extra place for your boss," her mother said. "I'm going to see if the water's boiling yet for the pasta."

Stephanie stood up and smoothed out her skirt, glad for an excuse to leave the room. Just as she headed for the kitchen, the front door flew open and she heard the rustling sounds of someone coming from the rain.

"Hey, anybody home?" her sister Angie called out. "Geez, it's wet out there. I sure hope to heck it doesn't rain like this on my wedding."

The remark made Stephanie smile as she walked out to greet her baby sister. Angie was wedding obsessed and could relate everything within the scope of her experience to the big day. A request to pass the salt, for instance, would make Angie think "Gee, I hope the caterer has enough salt shakers on the table at my wedding."

"It's going to be sunny and mild. I already told you. I checked the *Farmer's Almanac*." Stephanie gave Angie a hug, then kissed Jimmy Reilly, Angie's fiancé, on the cheek.

"Stop worrying, Angie. Man, you're driving me crazy," Jimmy said to his fiancée.

"That's what love is all about," Stephanie said brightly.

"Hey, whose car is that? Somebody win the lottery around here?"

Jimmy was referring to Matt's car, of course. Following the couple into the living room, Stephanie ducked her head, pretending she hadn't heard him.

Matt stood up and smiled, waiting to be introduced and Stephanie noticed her sister's eyes light up as they focused on him. The usual reaction he drew from women age eighteen to eighty.

Angie was engaged to be married, Stephanie reasoned, she wasn't dead.

Introductions were made all around and Stephanie explained how Matt had given her a ride to Brooklyn on his way out to his house in East Hampton.

"East Hampton...wow," her sister crooned. "It's so beautiful out there."

"It's a great place to get away. Very relaxing when you live in the city," Matt agreed with a polite smile.

"You staying for dinner?" Angie asked bluntly.

"Why...yes, I am."

"Great." She smiled at Matt and then at Stephanie in a way that made Stephanie want to strangle her.

"Let's go in the kitchen, Steph. I think Mom needs some help." Angie grabbed Stephanie's arm and tugged her along.

They'd barely stepped into the kitchen when Angie turned to her wide-eyed. "Oh my God! *That's* your boss? He is *totally* hot!"

Her shriek was *sotto voce,* but Stephanie still jumped forward and covered her sister's mouth with her hand.

"Shut up! He can hear you." She grabbed one of her mother's aprons that was hanging on a hook by the stove and tied it around her waist. "Here, grate this cheese. Mom needs some for the table."

Stephanie handed her sister a grater and a hunk of parmigiana cheese. Her mother always had a vast supply, but the job might occupy Angie enough to shut her up, Stephanie thought. Angie started grating while

Stephanie fished a strand of linguine out of the boiling water to test if it was done.

"So? Why the big secret? Why didn't you ever say your boss was a total hunk?"

Stephanie feigned an uncaring shrug. "I don't know...I guess I never really noticed."

Angie rolled her eyes and laughed. "I guess we'd better chip in and get you a guide dog for Christmas."

Stephanie smirked at her. "Great, I love dogs."

"Don't give me that look. Something's going on with that guy, right?" Angie prodded her.

"Not at all. We work together. You heard him."

"That's why he drives you all the way to Brooklyn in a rainstorm? Pretty cozy co-workers. Is that why you broke up with Tommy?"

Stephanie's jaw dropped. "Absolutely not...I mean, Matt is just my boss. Period. After next week, I'm going back to my old job and I won't be Matt's assistant anymore. And he has nothing to do with my breaking up with Tommy."

Angie set back to work on the cheese, grating quickly in a smooth rhythm, just as all the Rossi girls had been taught.

"Well, maybe I believe you and maybe not. If you are telling the truth and there is nothing cooking, I think you ought to seriously rethink the situation because that man is...awesome. A house in the Hamptons? And that car? Give me a break!"

Stephanie lowered the flame under the pasta pot. It was just about to boil over. Like her temper, she thought.

"Girls...what's going on in here?" Fran bustled in the kitchen. "What are you arguing about?"

Angie laughed. "I don't know why everyone says she's the smart one, Ma. Sometimes she's thick as a brick. She says she doesn't think her boss is good-looking."

"I never went that far," Stephanie retorted sharply.

Angie laughed. "Hah! *Gotcha!*"

The two sisters looked at each other and burst out laughing. Stephanie's mother lifted the cover on a large pot and checked the clam sauce.

"He seems like a very nice man, Stephanie. I heard him tell your father that's he's single. "

Oh, no, Stephanie thought. Her mother was usually her only ally in these matters. But now she was jumping into the act, too.

"Mom…please. He's just my boss."

"So? It's hard to meet a nice young man these days. And your father's right. You are a little too fussy, honey."

"Believe me, Mom. I'm not his type at all. He usually dates models and actresses. He doesn't want to…date me."

Take me to bed for a quick roll in the sheets, yes. Date me, no.

"Stephanie, you don't understand men," her mother insisted, stirring the sauce slowly. "Of course he likes to date these fast, flashy girls. But that doesn't mean he won't settle down with a nice girl from a good family, who knows how to cook and raise nice children…."

Stephanie stared at her mother. There was only one way to stop her when she got rolling on this topic of conversation.

"You'd better check the pasta, Mom. I think it's getting mushy…."

"For goodness' sake…let me see. Why didn't you girls watch it for me? You were standing right here…."

Fran quickly slipped out a strand and tasted it. "No, thank goodness. It's just right. Step aside, I'll strain it. You call everyone to the table, please. Dinner is ready."

Stephanie nodded. She paused and watched her mother lift the big pot of pasta and spill it into a stainless strainer in the sink.

As the steam clouds rose, Francesca masterfully shook out the extra water. Stephanie leaned over and kissed her cheek.

"What was that for?" her mother asked smiling with surprise.

"Just…because."

They drove her crazy sometimes. But she knew they only wanted the best for her and she did love them all insanely.

In the living room, the men were gathered around the TV, watching a baseball game and discussing the Yankees, her father's favorite topic, next to talking about his wife's cooking.

She hoped he wasn't boring Matt silly, but to the contrary, Matt seemed riveted by her father's stories of some former Yankee pitcher.

She announced that dinner was ready, but nobody seemed to notice. She walked around the room, collecting dirty dishes and wineglasses and piled them on a tray. Then she stood by her father, waiting for a break in his story.

"—he threw a knuckleball that was unhittable. Your eyes would cross trying to follow it through the air. We were just kids. We'd sneak into the ballpark and then as the game was going on, we'd work our way down the bleachers, until by the seventh inning, we were sitting right behind home plate. That was a view. Better than TV."

Matt laughed. "I love baseball but I hardly ever get to a game anymore. I have a box on the first base line, too. It's really a shame. Let me send you tickets sometime."

Dominic's eyes nearly popped out of his head. "You're pulling my leg, right? A box on the first base line? I'd think I died and went to heaven."

Stephanie stepped forward and gently took her father's arm. "If you don't sit down for dinner, you might make it up there before you know it, Dad. Mom is going to kill you if the food gets cold."

Her father laughed. He glanced over his shoulder at Matt. "She's got some sense of humor, this girl."

Matt met her eye a moment. "So I noticed."

Despite her strategies to sit on the opposite side of the table, Stephanie's mother managed to seat Stephanie at Matt's side.

Once everyone was seated, her father led the group in his usual, long rambling blessing, which included quiet thanks for the news that Nana Bella was safe and sound on a senior trip to Atlantic City, for the good food and the good company, ". . . including Stephanie's boss, Matthew here, who was so nice to drive her home in the rain," her father noted to the heavens in his conversational way.

Matt took a few bites and praised her mother lavishly. "You're right, Dominic. This is the best clam sauce I ever tasted."

"Didn't I tell you?" her father heartily agreed.

With the crisis of Nana's disappearance more or less resolved, the dinner conversation focused mostly on

Angie and Jimmy's wedding. Although all the plans were set, there were still a million last-minute details to take care of.

Stephanie had heard it all before. Not only with Angie's wedding, but with the three sisters who had already been married before her, Mary Ann, Christine and Gina.

Stephanie didn't talk much with Matt, despite their proximity. Or, maybe because of it, she thought later. It was hard to sit that close to him, feeling as if everyone in her family was watching them, thinking they were a couple...or should be.

She barely ate a bite of her mother's delicious meal and couldn't wait for the entire debacle to be over.

Just as it seemed Matt was getting ready to go, her sister Christine showed up with her husband Kevin in tow. They'd decided to drop by for coffee, offering support for the crisis with Nana and a box of Italian pastries from her father's favorite shop.

Of course, her parents insisted Matt stay for coffee and dessert. He couldn't—or wouldn't—pass up a chance to taste the best cannoli in Brooklyn.

Finally, dinner was done. Stephanie was the first to jump out of her chair and begin clearing the table.

"Well, I guess I'd better be on my way," she heard Matt say to her parents. "Fran, Dominic...thank you so much for your wonderful hospitality."

"You're very welcome, son. You come back and see us anytime." Her father slapped Matt on the back as he walked with him to the front door.

Her mother followed a few steps behind. "So glad you could stay. It was a pleasure meeting you, Matthew."

"The pleasure was all mine, honestly. Great food

and wonderful company. Who could beat that?" Matt's simple, polite reply was delivered with grave sincerity, Stephanie noticed. You could almost believe that he really meant it.

Well, it must have been an amusing evening for him, she reflected. Something like being an anthropologist, observing an exotic tribe. Or stepping into an episode of reality TV, *Growing Up Rossi.*

As Matt shrugged into his sports coat, her mother tugged on her father's sleeve. "Dom, come help me in the kitchen. I think the sink is clogged again…."

Stephanie saw her mother raise her eyebrows and give her father their not-so-secret sign.

"Oh…sure thing, Fran. Let me take a look."

Suddenly she was left alone with Matt in the foyer.

He gazed down at her, a sexy smile tugging at the corner of his mouth. "I know you didn't want me to stay nearly this long, Stephanie," he confided quietly. "But I didn't want to insult your parents."

"So I noticed. You did a good job. I think they're considering adoption. My father always wanted a son with a box at Yankee stadium," she whispered back.

The corner of his mouth turned up in that half smile that really got her. "If dinners like that are part of the deal, I just might consider it."

He gazed down at her with a mysterious, teasing grin. "Just for the record, do you really know how to cook?"

Her breath caught in her throat. She willed herself to pull her gaze away from his dark eyes, but couldn't.

His smile grew wider, tiny lines fanning out at the corners of his eyes. "On second thought, don't answer that. I'm not sure I want to know…."

He leaned over and planted a quick, hard kiss on her mouth. Stephanie leaned toward him, taken by surprise. Her hands moved up and rested on his chest. She felt her mouth relax slowly under his as his hands come around to circle her waist, pulling her closer.

They may have been standing there for ten seconds or ten minutes, she wasn't quite sure. Her head was spinning, her senses swimming in a sea of sensual delight.

Her logical brain scolded her, "Stephanie, stop it this instant! You swore you weren't going to get involved with him again."

Her illogical brain answered, "Oh...just shut up and mind your own business...will you please?"

While the two sides of her personality debated, the kiss went on and on. Who knows what would have happened next.

A sudden, ear-splitting sound broke into her sweet dream. A clatter from the kitchen sounded like a pile of pots falling on the floor. Stephanie jumped back, feeling dazed and confused. Her legs felt like rubber.

What was happening here? How had he managed to kiss her like that again? Why had she let him?

Matt stepped back, too, looking almost as shaken and surprised as she felt. Finally, he turned and opened the door.

"Well...good night. See you Monday. Have a nice weekend."

"Yes...good night." She watched him hop down the front steps, then start his car and pull away.

She stepped back in the house and closed the door. Angie stood nearby, wearing a knowing expression. She leaned on the wall and crossed her arms over her chest.

"So, is that how co-workers say good night in your office? *Mamma mia*…" Angie theatrically made the sign of the cross.

Stephanie stared at her younger sister a long moment, quelling her temper.

"Angie…I've been meaning to tell you something all night…I think there's something really icky stuck on your engagement ring. Tomato sauce, maybe?"

Her sister looked panicked. She flashed on the switch, and held up her hand up towards the light. "Where? Where did you see sauce?"

Stephanie slowly slipped upstairs, heading toward her old bedroom, now a guest room, where she'd be spending the night.

"I swear I saw something," she insisted in retreat. "Honest. I'm not kidding. You'd better check that. It can work itself right into the setting…."

Angie scowled at her, considering some rebuttal, Stephanie was sure. Then she ran off toward the kitchen.

"Mom? Do you have any jewelry cleaner?" Stephanie heard her whine.

It was mean but…she deserved it, Stephanie thought with a secret grin. She still had certain rights as an older sister.

Chapter Nine

The weekend passed much faster than Stephanie expected. She was immersed in Angie's last-minute wedding chores and the surprising twists and turns of Nana Bella's misadventures.

Although the family confirmed that Nana had checked into the Taj Mahal Casino and Hotel with the senior group from St. Anthony's Church, Nana would not return any of her son's phone calls.

When the bus carrying the Golden Age Club returned to Brooklyn on Sunday afternoon, Dominic Rossi was there to meet it. Stephanie stood alongside him in the church parking lot. She had come to give her father support and also to serve as a buffer for her grandmother. She searched the faces, one by one, as seniors stepped off the bus. No Nana Bella. Once again, her grandmother was missing in action.

Rosalie Trento, her grandmother's best friend, was the last off the bus. Dominic ran up to her. "Rose…where's my mother? Why isn't she on this bus?"

Rosalie looked him up and down with disdain. "Dominic Rossi…I know you since you were in diapers. You still stink. You should be ashamed of yourself."

Then the old woman stuck her tongue between her dentures and gave Dominic a long, noisy raspberry.

Her father stood back on his heels, shocked by the old lady's rebuke. Rosalie's daughter Maria ran up beside them and led her mother away by her arm.

"Sorry, Dom…Mama, that wasn't very nice," Stephanie heard her scold Rosalie.

Rose shrugged and clutched her tote bag a bit tighter under her arm. "You should hear what Bella says. He has it coming to him."

Meanwhile Stephanie's father jumped on the empty bus, which seemed about to drive away. "Hey, where do you think you're going? Where the hell is my mother?" he yelled at the bus driver.

"How do I know, buddy? All these old ladies look the same to me. Talk to that one, with the red hair. She's in charge."

The driver pointed to a woman in her midsixties who trotted around the parking lot on high heel slides, carrying a clipboard. She wore black capri pants and an oversized T-shirt that said Lucky Lady in gold glitter script. A big, lipstick-covered smile and a sticker on her shoulder that read, Welcome! My name is: Lucille Weigers! completed the look.

"I'm looking for my mother, Bella Rossi. She's supposed to be on this bus," Dominic said as he clambered back down to the parking lot. Stephanie could tell her father was trying not to yell, but his voice rose a few decibels with every word.

"Now, now, calm down, sir. There must be some mistake," Lucille Weigers soothed in a practiced tour-guide tone.

"No mistake. She left on Friday, due back on Sunday. On this bus!" Dominic jabbed his finger at the empty bus. "What, did you leave her at a rest stop or something?"

Lucille lifted a pair of reading glasses that hung from a chain around her neck and checked her clipboard. "Let's see…Bella Rossi…." She flipped a sheet, keeping both Stephanie and her father frozen in suspense. "Here we go. You're right. Mrs. Rossi was due to return this afternoon, but she decided to extend her stay. They do enjoy themselves so much." Lucille grinned. "It's just harmless fun. Keeps the old ticker going. As long as they don't dump the whole Social Security check, you know…."

Stephanie thought her father was going to have a stroke. His face turned beet-red, then grew pale as paper. He seemed to be trembling with anger, and couldn't speak.

"Dad?" She took his arm. "Come over here and sit down a minute. You don't look well."

"Sit down? How can I sit down at a time like this?" He shook off her arm and pressed a hand to his chest, as if in pain. "Your grandmother is wandering all over Jersey! That Rose Trento! She's a bad influence. She runs with a fast crowd, that one…."

Stephanie rolled her eyes. Rose didn't use a walker yet, if that's what he meant.

"Why didn't your grandmother come home on that bus? Maybe she's sick and she's too stubborn to call us!"

"Dad, calm down. Nana's not sick. She's just having a good time. She probably just needed a break from the routine. You said it yourself. She'll be back in a day or two. Why don't we go home and try calling her again? Maybe she'll answer this time."

Her father didn't reply. He looked stunned, staring out into the now empty parking lot. The bus gunned its engine and pulled away in a cloud of exhaust.

"That's it," her father said finally. "This baloney has gone far enough!"

Stephanie didn't answer. When she was a little girl, she and her sisters always knew their father had reached his limit with bad behavior when her father shouted up those very words, his famous battle cry, "This baloney has gone far enough!"

"I'm driving down to Atlantic City right now, and I'll bring her back home tonight. She's seventy-seven years old. She can't be running around like a teenager. Maybe she's got a screw loose or something." He turned to Stephanie. "Maybe she's got that Old Timers disease."

"Alzheimer's you mean?"

"That's it. They say people do strange things. They wander off. You can't reason with them."

"Trust me, Dad. Nana is sharp as a tack. I think you should just let her wear herself out and come home when she's ready."

He glanced at her and huffed a long sigh. Then he patted Stephanie on the arm. "I know you mean well, honey. But you don't understand. She's not young anymore. She needs someone to look after her. She can't travel around like that on her own anymore. If something happened to her, God forbid, I'd never forgive myself. Come on, I'll drop you off at home and tell your mother what's what."

Stephanie followed him back to his car without comment. Back at home, she'd hoped her mother would talk some sense into her father, but Francesca was unsuccessful in dissuading him as well. A short time later, her father left the house again with a small overnight bag and a large tote bag full of food and a Thermos of coffee, continuing his Nana Bella "bring 'em back alive" bounty hunt.

Her mother watched from the window as the big Buick pulled down the street. "He's stubborn. And she is, too. Cut from the same cloth, what can I tell you?"

"Do you think he'll find Grandma?"

Her mother shook her head. "God only knows. He might find her...but that doesn't mean she'll come back. They really went at it on Friday, before she left. I don't think they ever had such an argument."

Stephanie had not found a chance to speak her mother privately about this all weekend and now wanted to hear the whole story. "What did they argue about, Mom? You never really told me."

"It started off very innocently. We were sitting at breakfast. Your grandmother came down all dressed up, carrying the help wanted ads from the newspapers. She said she was going to look for a job. Your father laughed. 'Don't be crazy, Mom,' he said to her. 'Who's going to hire a woman your age?' Well, that hurt her feelings. You could see it in her face. I see seniors working everywhere these days and I told him so. Your grandmother is in good health and she's very active. She loves to talk to people, God knows. She probably could get a job." Fran shook her head. "Your father is so old-fashioned. It's still hard for him to see women working outside of the house, no less a woman in her seventies. But what is she supposed to do all day? Sit around and watch soap operas? That's not even healthy."

Stephanie loved her father, but she wasn't blind to his shortcomings. He could be very old-fashioned and narrow-minded when it came to any issues that involved home life.

"Is that when Nana ran up to her room?"

Her mother shook her head. "No, there was more. Your grandmother said she was tired of living here and that she should have never sold her house and moved in with us. She said she felt smothered, and that your father treated her like a little girl, who was too young to even cross the street by herself. She said she was going to get her own apartment and find a job and have a life again. She also announced that she was going on a cruise with her sister Lily and maybe even Rose Trento. They want to see Alaska. She already put down a deposit. But that's not until the end of the summer. She's hoping to get some vacation time from her new job."

Stephanie's mother smiled wistfully at the final footnote.

"Well…that does sound serious. You didn't tell me half of this, Mom. No wonder she's not answering any phone calls. We're lucky she didn't run off to Alaska this weekend."

Her mother sighed. She nodded at Stephanie. "That's just what I said to your father. That's why I said, even if he finds her, she might not come back. And if she comes back, what then? There has to be some changes, Stephanie. I hoped when your grandmother ran off, it would sink in and he'd learn his lesson. But he doesn't want to face it."

Stephanie felt sorry for her mother, being caught in the middle, more or less, powerless to do anything. She patted her mother's hand. "We'll just have to wait and see. I know Nana wouldn't do anything to ruin Angie's wedding next weekend. Maybe the wedding will help them smooth things over."

"I hope so, honey. I hope so." Her mother glanced at her. "I know it's a lot to ask, Stephanie. But they both listen to you. Maybe when your grandmother comes back, you could help them work it out somehow?"

"Gee, Mom. I'm not sure what I can do. But of course, if I have the chance, I would try."

Her mother didn't say anything. She patted Stephanie's hand and forced a thin smile.

Stephanie didn't want to leave her mother alone on Sunday night. She waited with her for her father's return instead of going back to the city. He called once in the late afternoon to say he had arrived in Atlantic City and looked for Bella at her hotel, but she'd checked out. Once again, Stephanie's mother urged him to come home, but he insisted he would stay and keep looking, feeling sure Stephanie's grandmother couldn't have gone far.

Finally, at nearly midnight he called again. He had not found Bella. He was giving up for the night. He'd checked in at a motel and would resume the search again tomorrow.

Stephanie went to sleep in her old bedroom with a heavy heart. She hated to see her family in such an uproar, especially right before Angie's wedding. She felt empathy for her grandmother, knowing firsthand how smothering her father could be. But she also felt sympathy for her father. She knew he didn't mean to make his mother unhappy and only wanted Bella to live out the rest of her days in comfort and safety. Even if that meant keeping her under house arrest.

There didn't seem to be an easy solution. Though her mother seemed to expect she could negotiate one.

Stephanie rushed into work late on Monday morning feeling weary and irritable. The subway ride from Brooklyn had been fraught with delays and she'd been forced to switch trains twice to an alternate, roundabout route. She'd started the day scouring her sister Angie's closet for something to wear. She hadn't planned on staying over Sunday night and her suit from Friday was rumpled from the rain. Her younger sister's wardrobe fell into two distinct categories—dental assistant uniforms and MTV diva wannabe. Not only was Angie smaller and shorter, but also she wore her clothes tighter than Stephanie would ever dare. The challenge was daunting and she'd piled the bed high with outfits until she found one even vaguely suitable.

Her final choice was a summer weight suit which looked acceptable, compared to the rest. Its pale-pink color looked very innocent on the hanger. Almost like something in her own closet. But once she'd put it on, the skirt was short and tight with small slits on the side of each thigh to allow for walking. The wrap-style jacket belted at the waist with wide, rounded lapels, edged with fringe that draped in a deep V. The cut accentuated cleavage that didn't actually exist, Stephanie noticed. Sort of an optical fashion illusion, she decided.

Angie's high heels made matters even worse…or better. Depending on how you looked at it.

Stephanie left her parents' house feeling odd, as if she was in disguise, going to a costume party dressed as Barbie dressed as an executive...or a call girl working the day shift, however you wanted to look at it. The approving glances and blatant come-ons from her fellow commuters took her by surprise. She pretended to ignore them, all the while yanking her skirt hem with each step in a strange, staggering march down the sidewalk and into the hotel.

Once up in her office, she was in no mood to face Matt...or put up with more of his —his "avoid picking a replacement" game, for one thing. And certainly not his "kiss and run" seduction games. Merely an ego-boost thing for him, she'd decided. He just liked to rattle her cage, assure himself she was still attracted. It didn't mean anything.

The more she thought about it, the madder she got. He had some nerve kissing her like that on Friday night. After they'd both agreed not to get involved and put their unfortunate lapse of judgement behind them.

He was lucky that she showed up for work at all.

She snatched up the file of resumés for her replacement from her desk and decided to confront him, first thing. She'd make him pick some candidates to interview, or she'd pick the replacement herself.

No attractive young women need apply if she was choosing, she realized. She couldn't stand the idea of that. As much as she knew he wasn't right for her, and a real relationship would never work out. She couldn't leave here picturing him sweeping some other unsuspecting female off her feet.

As if it would make any difference. Stephanie sighed. The guy could barely walk down a city block without at least one or two gorgeous babes falling at his feet. She couldn't kid herself. He'd sideswiped her with a smoldering kiss Friday night, then probably spent the rest of the weekend at his beach house in some other woman's arms.

With the folder tucked firmly under her arm, she marched towards Matt's office. She knocked sharply on the half closed door and just barely waited for his call to come in.

"There you are...I didn't know you were in yet."

Matt greeted her with a dazzling smile. Then his eyebrows rose a notch as he looked her over head to toe, taking in her fashion-doll outfit with a smoldering glance. She fought the urge to show any reaction or yank on her skirt hem. It took a moment for her to realize they weren't alone.

Someone sat in a chair directly facing his desk. The chair was turned away from her and she couldn't see the person's face. Only an orange baseball cap and the tip of one large white sneaker, with Velcro fasteners. The flowery perfume, that smelled so familiar...

"Hi, honey. We were waiting for you. What, did you get stuck on the subway?" The visitor rose and twisted around to face her. "My, don't you look pretty in pink today."

Stephanie felt her mouth drop open. "Nana...what are you doing here?"

Nana Bella shot her a perky smile. "I just got in from AC. I didn't mean to bother you at work, sweetie, but I told them at the front desk who I was and they let me come up to see you. Your boss found me hanging around and he invited me to wait in here."

"Really, how thoughtful." Stephanie met Matt's

innocent stare. She wondered why he felt inspired to en-
tertain her grandmother, but decided to worry about
that later.

"I stopped by your apartment this morning. I must
have just missed you. I thought I'd wait there till you
got home, but your super wouldn't let me in. Didn't
believe I was your grandmother." Bella laughed and
shook her head. "The guy must need glasses. She looks
just like me, don't you think?"

Nana Bella directed her question to Matt, who
seemed to hang on her every word. "Spitting image.
Like sisters," he said agreeably.

Bella giggled and waved her hand at him. "Oh boy, this
fella's a smooth operator," she said to Stephanie. "You
better watch out. He could charm a dog off a meat wagon."

Woof-woof, she wanted to say aloud.

She leaned forward and gave her grandmother a
quick hug. "Nana…we were so worried about you.
Why didn't you call?"

Nana Bella shrugged. "I'm sorry. You're right. I
should have called the house. But your father got me
too p.o.'d this time. I might as well be dead and buried
the way he treats me. I wanted to look for a job and he
acted like I'd lost my marbles. A nice little job in the
neighborhood. Part-time, just to get out and see people
a little. What's so crazy with that? I'm not talking about
taking over IBM…."

"Sure. I understand." Stephanie sighed and glanced
at Matt. He didn't need to hear all this, although he certainly seemed interested. "Nana, why don't you come
into my office? We can talk some more. Privately. I'm
sure Mr. Harding has work to do."

"Oh. Sure, honey. Sorry for shooting my mouth off

and airing the family laundry, Matt," Bella said to Matt. So they were on a first-name basis already? He did work fast, Stephanie noticed.

"It was delightful to meet you, Bella. Drop by any time. If you're serious about finding a job, maybe I can help you."

Stephanie felt her stomach drop. Was he actually offering her grandmother a job? Was he out of his mind?

"Here, in your hotel you mean?" Nana asked eagerly. "I lived in New York City my whole life. I know the city like the back of my hand. I'd be great as a tour guide or something in that general direction."

Matt laughed. "I think you would be, too." He glanced at Stephanie, fending off the daggers in her dark eyes. "I think your grandmother would be a great addition to our staff. She could answer questions at the visitors desk. We have a lot of senior groups booking in lately. She's someone that can really relate to that market."

Stephanie didn't reply. All she knew was the sooner she got Nana Bella out his office, the better. Unless he was considering her grandmother for her own replacement....

"Thanks, Matt. I hope you're not just talking off the top of your head now, because I'm going to take you up on that," she warned him.

"Any time, Bella. You just call me." Nana Bella gave Matt a hearty handshake. Then she grabbed the handle of her large, rolling suitcase, dragging it behind her like a faithful pet as she followed Stephanie to the door.

"Let me help you with that." Stephanie grabbed for the suitcase leash but Nana insisted on doing it herself.

"I'm okay, honey. I like rolling this thing along. I think it's my Gypsy blood, kicking in."

"I didn't know we were related to any Gypsies, Nana."

"Well, not exactly. But I had a great aunt, could tell your fortune with a drop of olive oil in a bowl of water. She was *almost* a Gypsy." Nana huffed.

Stephanie glanced over her shoulder and caught Matt's glance. His dark eyes danced with amusement, a sexy dimple creased one cheek and a corner of his wide mouth turned up into a reluctant, totally charming grin.

She turned away, and released a long sigh. She didn't know whether she wanted to smack him…or kiss him.

It was shaping up to be a hell of a Monday.

Stephanie let her grandmother into her own office and shut the door. She took a few deep calming breaths as Nana Bella gazed around.

"Nice office, Stephanie. But very impressive. You're really moving up the ladder, honey. Aren't you?"

She was. Except for slipping off the ladder into her boss's bed.

"Thanks, Nana. Why don't you sit down, make yourself comfortable a minute and we'll talk."

Nana Bella sat down on a leather armchair and Stephanie sat next to her. "Boy oh boy…that's some boss you got there. He's even better-looking than those guys on the soap operas. And he's a very nice fellow, too. Very respectful." She nodded in approval. "I'm going to take him up on that job offer."

Stephanie didn't even want to deal with the situation yet. "Yes, he's very…nice," she agreed distractedly.

Nana leaned closer, her voice lowered. "Is he single?"

"Uh...yes...I mean, no...I mean, I'm not really sure....

Listen Nana, why did you go to my apartment this morning? Why didn't you just go home to Brooklyn? You know Dad drove out to Atlantic City yesterday to look for you. I bet he's still there."

Nana looked surprised. Then amused. But not the least bit contrite, Stephanie noticed.

"Well, that sounds about right. I guess he was planning on bringing me back, dead or alive, like one of those bounty hunters on TV."

"Nana, please. He was worried about you."

"I know. But your father goes a little overboard sometimes. He's what you'd call a type A personality. I read about it in a magazine. He's going to give himself a heart attack one of these days. He ought to calm down and go with the flow a little, you know what I mean?"

Stephanie had to smile. "Yes, I do."

"I'm not going back to Sackett Street, Stephanie. I mean it. I'm going to find myself a little apartment someplace and a little job and have a life. I'm healthy as a horse, thank God, and I still have some brains in my head. I even have a little money in the bank. It ain't over till the fat lady sings, you know what I mean?"

Stephanie nodded. Her grandmother was trying to live her life fully, down to the wire. Who could fault her for that?

"I understand...so, you're not going back to Brooklyn, is that it?"

Nana nodded hard. "You got it. If you can't put me up a few days, until I find my own place, that's okay. I'll stay in a hotel or something."

"Don't be silly. Of course you can stay with me." At

least the family would know that Nana was safe and sound. She'd give her father a few days to calm down, then let them sort things out. Hopefully in time for Angie's wedding next weekend.

"We'll have fun together, honey. I always wanted to be single in the city." Her grandmother grinned and winked at her.

Stephanie laughed. "Believe me, Nana. It's not all it's cracked up to be."

Nana stood up and rubbed her hands together. "We'll see about that."

Stephanie called the super in her building to clear the way for Nana Bella. She gave her grandmother keys to her apartment, escorted her downstairs and packed her into a taxi.

Back up in her office, she called her mother and reported the goods news; Nana was alive and well, and now hiding out in her apartment.

"I know Daddy. As soon as he hears, he'll race in to take her home. But you have to tell him that will only make it worse. She won't go. At least, not yet. I think they both need a few days to cool off," Stephanie warned.

"Yes, you're right. I'll make sure he gives her a little breathing room. Otherwise, she might take off again for God only knows where."

Stephanie promised to keep her mother updated and soon finished the call. She sat back and looked over her desk, trying to get her bearings. The morning's domestic drama had exhausted her, but she still had piles of work to do. Lots to prepare for her replacement. She still needed to confront Matt about picking her replacement, for one thing. Once again, she picked up the folder of resumés and headed for his office. His secretary

Margaret Waters was on the phone and signaled that he was free.

Stephanie stood by the half-open door and Matt waved her in. He stood by his desk, stuffing papers into his briefcase.

"Back so soon? Do you miss me?" She ignored his teasing grin and kept a serious expression.

"Did you have a chance to look at the candidates for my replacement? I really need to set up some interviews."

He glanced at the file she held out, but didn't make a move to take it from her. "Oh…that. Sure. I have the copy you gave me around here somewhere…." He sifted through some papers on his desk. "Maybe I left it out at the house this weekend—"

"Here, take mine." Stephanie stuck the file into his briefcase. "I've marked the most likely possibilities. I can set up one or two interviews for this afternoon if you're free."

"Sorry, that won't work out for me. I'm on my way to Boston, an emergency meeting with the architects at the new property. Care to come along? You might enjoy it," he promised, a glint in his eye.

Right, just like the last emergency business trip I took with you. Fool me once, shame on you. Fool me twice….

"Thanks, but I'm going to pass. I have a lot to do around here. Since I am leaving at the end of the week," she added curtly.

She thought he might have winced at the reminder, but he turned away from her quickly to snap closed his briefcase.

"And I guess you do need to stay in the city now for your grandmother." He sifted through some papers on his desk. "I've been thinking about a job for her. The visitors desk would be a good place, don't you think?"

Stephanie looked at him, her head tilted to one side. "Frankly, I didn't think you were serious about that."

He looked up at her, his dark eyes wide with a guileless expression. "Now, why wouldn't I have been serious? She's personable and charming and she's a genuine, native New Yorker. She could certainly answer tourist questions a few hours a week. Besides, if she's determined to get out in the work force again, don't you think it's best to have her here, a safe environment, where you can keep an eye on her? I think your family would prefer that solution, too."

Now he was even taking her family's feeling into consideration? Stephanie was so surprised, she couldn't reply.

"Well, you've thought this over pretty thoroughly, haven't you?"

"Yes, pretty much. What's the matter? I thought you'd be pleased. It solves a big problem."

"I am pleased. It does make sense and entirely solves the problem."

"But...?" He watched her with a curious expression, waiting to see what she'd say next.

She paused and took a breath. "You don't have to be so...nice to me, Matt. I think you feel guilty about last weekend and believe me, there's no reason for it. I'm a big girl. I knew what I was doing."

He looked confused for a moment by her admission. Then amused. "No argument there. You definitely knew what you were doing, Stephanie."

He leaned back on the edge of his desk, his arms crossed over his chest. His gaze telegraphed an intimate message, forcing her to remember their intimate moments. Stephanie felt her defenses melting, then forced herself to look away.

Why did he have to be so...impossible. "Look, can't we just discuss this like adults? Without the clever comments."

He gave her an innocent look. "I wasn't trying to be clever, just stating a simple fact. Besides, I was the one who suggested that we talk the other day. You said there was nothing to talk about."

She sniffed and crossed her arms over her chest. "Well...maybe there wasn't then. But there is now. I don't want any special handling, Matt. I want you to treat me the way you always did. Before last weekend, I mean."

He sat at the edge of his desk, his gaze fixed on her. "Which was?"

"If you felt like shouting your head off at me, you just did. You didn't worry about my feelings all the time. Or what I thought. You treated me like I was just...a piece of furniture or your computer terminal. Not so personal. Not so patient and...nice."

Now he did wince and didn't try to hide it. "You think I treated you like a piece of furniture?"

Stephanie sighed. This was a hard conversation, but it had to be said.

"Well...yes. Pretty much. Don't get me wrong," she rushed to add. "I didn't really hold it against you. I'm not even saying I wanted it differently. In fact, for the few days remaining, I hope you'll act the same way."

He looked down at the carpet a second, considering her request. Then finally back up at her, his chiseled features set in an unreadable expression. "I'm sorry,

Stephanie. But I can't do that. Not even if I wanted to. Like it or not, our relationship is different now. You just told me you knew what you were doing. Well, you crossed a line that night, for better or worse. We can pretend nothing happened. But we can't go back."

He looked as if he was about to say something more. Then his expression changed. He stared at her. While he didn't make a move to come closer she could feel the air between them sizzle, charged with energy. She felt her body listing toward him, pulled in by some invisible force. It would have been so easy to step just a few inches closer and feel his strong arms wrap around her again….

Hold it right there! She sent herself a mental splash of cold water and took a quick step back.

"You'll just have to put up with my being *nice* to you for a few more days. I hope you can stand it."

Stephanie didn't know what to say. Had she really hurt his feelings? He was acting as if she had, yet she couldn't quite believe it.

"I'll see you tomorrow then. If anything comes up, you know where to reach me." He grabbed his suit jacket from the back of his chair and slipped it on. He glanced at her, a dismissing look. She wondered if she should apologize.

No, she decided. It was better to leave it this way.

Chapter Ten

Nana Bella primped before the mirror in the women's employee dressing room, obviously pleased with her reflection.

"So, what do you think? Not so bad for an old lady, right?"

"Nana...you look great. Very...official." Stephanie stepped over and smoothed the jacket of Nana's new uniform.

"I'll say. I think this outfit takes off ten pounds. And ten years. At least."

Stephanie had to agree again. Nana looked suddenly slimmer and younger, but it was possibly owing as much to the sparkle in her eye and the spring in her step as any magic from her new outfit.

"I have to tell you, honey, I'm a little nervous. First

day on the job and all." Nana shook her head and smiled. "It's been a long time."

Stephanie touched her hand. "You don't have to go through with this if you don't want to, Nana. It's okay. Everyone will understand."

Nana looked shocked by the suggestion. "What me, chicken out? No way, baby. I never let a few butterflies in my tummy stand in my way." She took a deep breath and fluffed the silver-gray curls on her head with the tip of her tail comb...for at least the tenth time, Stephanie noticed. "Besides, I don't want to embarrass you in front of your boss."

"Oh...don't worry about him." She glanced at her grandmother and quickly looked away.

"What do you think, I'm blind? I know the only reason he found a job for me is because he's got a sweet spot for you, *bella*."

Stephanie felt herself blushing. Nana's inquisitive gaze made matters even worse. "Don't be silly, Nana. He's just my boss. He doesn't have any special feeling for me."

"You can't fool your grandmother. I've been around a long time. I know what I see between a man and woman. It's an old story, Stephanie. Older even than me. When you walked into that room, his eyes were eating you up...and you were the same way," she added. She paused, catching Stephanie's eye even though she tried to look away. "When that lightning strikes, there's nothing you can do."

Stephanie shook her head. Nana's observations had hit a bull's eye and it was hard to deny any of it.

"Nana...let's just say that even if that's true, nothing is going to come of it. So I'd rather not talk about it. Not even with you. Okay?"

Nana glanced at her and patted her hand. "Whatever

you say, my lovely. It's just between you and me, right?"

Stephanie nodded. "Right." She smiled and changed the subject. "So, did you tell your friend Rosalie about your new job?"

Nana grinned. "You bet I did. She was so jealous, she was doing a tap dance."

"Well, you can call her tonight and give a full report. Today will just be training and orientation. Just see how it goes. I don't want you to overdo."

"I'm going to love it," Nana promised her.

Stephanie thought so, too. She hoped she hadn't made an mistake by encouraging her grandmother. More than encouraging her, "aiding and abetting" her father had accused her, as if Nana going to work again was possibly a federal offense.

"Ready to get out there?" Nana glanced at her watch. "I don't want to be late my first day on the job."

"Yes, we're ready. Oh, wait. I nearly forgot. One more thing…" Stephanie reached into her pocket and took out a slim gold nameplate engraved with the name, Bella Rossi. She reached over and pinned it on the pocket of Nana's navy blue blazer.

"There you go. Now you're all set."

Nana touched the nameplate with her fingertips and leaned closer to the mirror to get a better look. "Wow. I'm a real working girl now."

"Yes." Stephanie laughed. "Looks like it's official."

Nana turned to her. "Thank you, sweetheart. Thank you for doing this for me. I feel like…like I'm a person again. Like I'm not invisible anymore."

Before Stephanie could answer, her grandmother

leaned over and gave her a tight hug. Then she quickly stepped back.

"You're a good girl, Stephanie. I'm going to stop in church tonight and light a candle for you. For you…and Mr. Lightning Bolt."

Stephanie shook her head. She didn't know whether to laugh or cry. "Oh Nana…come on. Enough of this crazy talk. Let's not be late for your big debut."

Taking her grandmother by the hand, she led her out of the changing room and into the first day of Nana's new career. Delivering Nana to her new supervisor, Gloria Nesbit, Manager of Guest Services. Gloria was pleasant, but very professional and expert with training new employees. Stephanie expected that if her grandmother was capable of doing this job, Gloria would whip Nana into shape in no time.

Leaving Nana just outside the training room door, Stephanie went up to her own office. She felt as she'd just left a child to the first day of school. It certainly was a new phase in Nana's life and an inspiring lesson to Stephanie that it's never too late to have a dream and go after it.

Her family, particularly her father, did not feel the same. The Rossi women were evenly divided, with Stephanie, Angie and Mary Ann taking their grandmother's side. Christine and Gina, along with her mother, sided with their father.

Dominic had hit the roof when he'd heard his mother had found a job at the hotel. Of course, he'd blamed Stephanie. But she'd calmly convinced him that Nana was determined to work somewhere and it might as well be in a pleasant atmosphere where she was close at hand. Just as Matt had predicted, the argument had appeased her family. For now at least.

Finally, there was nothing her father could do to prevent it. Nana had only spoken to him once on the phone so far from Stephanie's apartment, and when he tried to visit her on Tuesday, she wouldn't let him in.

Meanwhile, Stephanie had been doing her best to act as an intermediary between the two feuding factions. Her parents were distracted right now by Angie's wedding, coming up in only a few days, which definitely took the heat off her grandmother. Next week would be a different story and Stephanie braced herself, knowing things would soon come to a head between her father and grandmother.

So far at least, the conflict had not affected her grandmother's plans to attend Angie's wedding. Nana didn't want to ruin Angie's day, she'd told Stephanie, and promised to be on her best behavior. These days, it was hard to tell what Nana's best behavior was, and Stephanie hoped there wouldn't be any major family scenes. Even so, she knew the whole family would be talking about the way Nana had run away from home and her battle with Dominic.

But at least the aunts, uncles and cousins won't be gossiping as much about me not having a date for the wedding, she'd realized. So there was some upside to the situation after all.

Secretly, she did feel bad about attending such a major event without an escort. In darker moments, it made her feel everyone would be pitying her, thinking she was a real loser. It was bad enough that she'd dated Tommy for years before he'd proposed. Her family saw her as "the career girl" who shunned their values and traditions. But Stephanie knew she was hardly the radical feminist they made her out to be. She did want to fall madly in love, marry and have children and do all those things that seemed so expected. But she knew in her heart that marrying Tommy wouldn't have been the right choice. She wasn't going to marry someone just for the sake of being married. She gave herself credit for making a hard decision. Though it seemed that nobody else did.

To make matters even worse, Tommy would be at the wedding, too. The Torrellis and Rossis were close friends and even if the invitations hadn't been sent out before the split, it would have been unthinkable to exclude him. Her friends said he should have been a good sport and not accepted, all things considered. But Tommy wasn't in a good sport mood lately, Stephanie had learned.

Angie had heard he was still angry at Stephanie for dumping him, and was flaunting a new girlfriend around the neighborhood. "A real bombshell type," Angie had described her, rolling her eyes. Coming from Angie, Queen of the Tight Skirts and Stiletto Heels, Stephanie knew that was saying something. Stephanie pictured the works—dyed blond hair, big boobs, collagen-puffed lips. Every man's fantasy. Probably brainless, she tried to comfort herself, cold comfort though it was.

Word on the street reported that Tommy was bringing the Bombshell to the wedding, a transparent, immature ploy to hurt Stephanie's feelings. Humiliate her, or make her jealous. Or all three.

As if she didn't have enough to handle that day. Stephanie thought she might try to find a sequined neck brace to wear with her fancy dress so that she'd be sure to keep her head up high all night.

She fantasized about skipping the whole thing—feigning a sudden dreadful illness or accident. But she couldn't let her sister down. Or her parents. Besides, she wasn't a coward. If Nana could start a job at age seventy-seven, she could face down Tommy Torrelli and his bimbo wedding date.

It was one day. One lousy day in her life. She could last through it, she promised herself. She wasn't going to drive herself crazy over this…though she probably needed a much sexier outfit if she was going to survive with any shred of pride intact.

Maybe she'd go shopping after work tonight. Tomorrow night was the rehearsal dinner and then only two more days to the wedding. Buying a dress for Angie's wedding was becoming her new hobby, she realized. She already had three possible outfits hanging in her closet. Yet none of them seemed quite right. She grabbed a yellow Post-it and scribbled Shop for *sexier* dress. ASAP! then stuck it on her computer terminal. Then she forced herself to focus on the piles of work spread over her desk.

At least Matt hadn't been around all week. She'd expected him back in the office from Boston on Tuesday, but he'd sent her a short e-mail, stating he had to fly down to Atlanta for some other emergency. While his being out of the office solved one problem, her awkwardness in dealing with him since their one-night fling, it created another in that he wasn't around to choose her replacement. Stephanie was starting to think that wasn't her problem. She'd given him ample warning and a stack of resumés. The ball was in his court now.

If only it was all that simple. As the days dwindled in her two-week countdown, she wished she could feel happy and relieved that the ordeal would soon be over.

But she wasn't.

Not seeing him for a few days in a row had caused a painful kind of withdrawal. She found herself sighing a lot, staring off into space, picturing his face or the sound of his voice. The way he looked at her sometimes when she thought she wasn't looking.

The way he could smile at her and set her on fire inside.

She sighed aloud. Well, she just had to get used to it. The sooner the better, she told herself. As of Friday, she was out of this office and maybe even working out a transfer to another hotel in the chain. While that did seem a bit extreme, Stephanie now thought it might be the only way to cure herself from this…madness. She'd never quite felt like this about anyone before, a feverish thing. A hunger. An ache in her bones.

Lightning had struck all right. Just as Nana had said. But it had burned her badly. Matthew Harding wasn't going to be the man to give her the future she'd imagined for herself. He could give her a wild, passionate affair that would leave her even more hurt and baffled than she felt already. But he wasn't going to be the one to walk her up the aisle at St. Anthony's and leave all her relatives—for once—without a thing to say about her.

Except that she made a beautiful bride.

Stephanie shook the fuzzy daydream from her brain. She turned to her computer terminal and tried to focus on the screen, a forecast of guest occupancy for what appeared to be the next…millennium.

The numbers swam before her eyes and she knew that trying to make any sense of the report right now was useless. She checked her watch. Just about twelve, a respectable hour for a lunch break. Nana was having lunch in her training session. Stephanie felt free to head out into the city streets and do what most women would do when the emotional burdens of family feuds, angry ex-fiancés, potential public humiliation and undeniable passion for a womanizing boss weighed them down.

She decided to go shopping.

"So after lunch we did a play-acting thing. One person would pretend to be a hotel guest, asking sight-seeing questions, and the other person had to be the Visitor Information Representative…." Nana Bella was so animated as she related the details of her day, she had to pause to take a long breath.

Her bright-pink lipstick was faded, her name plate was hanging a bit askew, but her eyes glowed with vitality; a good sign, Stephanie thought. A very good sign.

"Now this wasn't as easy as it sounds. Gloria would act like the customer and she threw us plenty of curves. And she could get pretty nasty. You had to keep smiling and keep a lid on, if you know what I mean." Nana nodded. "You know my temper, *bella*. That's not so easy for your grandmother."

Stephanie grinned. At least Nana was honest enough to admit it. "How did you do?"

Nana sat back, her head lifted proudly. "I did pretty darned good. Gloria says at this rate, she might start me on Friday."

Stephanie leaned over and gave her grandmother a quick hug. "That's great, Nana. I'm so proud of you."

"Thanks, honey. I'm proud, too. I was thinking we should go out and celebrate. Maybe that restaurant on the corner near your apartment. Siam Palace?"

"Nana, that's Thai food." Stephanie had rarely

known her grandmother to dine out. Maybe some cozy Italian café, where the most challenging dish was fried calamari. But never an Asian restaurant.

"I know. But I'm up for trying something new. It smells so good when I pass by. I can tell they're cooking with a lot of garlic. There's got to be something in there I'd like to eat."

"Okay, if you say so. Thai food it is. Just give me a minute to straighten off my desk and we can go."

"So, how was your day?" Nana smiled at her with interest. "Did that good-looking boss of yours come back from his trip?"

Stephanie shrugged. "Not that I know of."

Nana gave her a look. "Don't try that with me, sweetie. I know you'd know. There's a certain kind of moth that can smell its mate five hundred miles away. I'm not kidding. I saw it on a nature show."

Stephanie shook her head, sorting out the memos in her in box. "Nana, what does that have to do with anything?"

Nana shrugged and gave her an innocent look. "I'm just making conversation. Nature is powerful. Don't you think that's interesting?"

"Fascinating," Stephanie replied drily.

Nana was quiet for a moment, glancing around Stephanie's office as she waited. "Wow, Bloomingdale's," she said, reading the large shopping bag that stood in the corner of the room. "Looks like somebody went shopping today."

Stephanie glanced up at her. "I got a dress for Angie's wedding."

"Another one? You got enough now for Cher's farewell tour."

"Nana…" Stephanie shook her head. Where did she

come up with these things? "I'm going to bring the rest back. This is the one. Not too sedate. Not too...too."

"Can I see?" Nana picked up the bag and peeked inside. "Oh my, very nice fabric. Sort of sheer and...flimsy."

"It's silk chiffon. It's that handkerchief sort of thing with all the layers. You can't really tell what it looks like on the hanger."

Nana took the dress all the way out of the bag. She clutched her throat with her other hand. "*Madonna mia*...did you pay the full price, *bella?*"

Stephanie swallowed. The dress had been pricey, discovered in one of the little designer salon sections that she usually found so intimidating. But bolstered by the prospect of facing down Tommy's Bimbo Date, Stephanie screwed up her courage and decided that price was no object.

"It's a Cara Spark original, Nana. You have to pay a lot for designer styles." She held the dress up against her bland, tan linen suit.

Nana hesitated a moment. "You try it on for me, honey. I can't tell anything like that."

Stephanie considered waiting until they got home, then decided she couldn't stand the suspense. It was hard to shop for such an important occasion all alone and she did want a second opinion. She was also dying to try on the dress again and see if it was really as fabulous-looking as she'd thought.

"Okay, just give me a second." With the dress in hand, she slipped into her private bathroom and quickly changed. She stepped out and did a model-like catwalk across the office carpeting toward her grandmother.

"I'd need some really high heels, I guess," she said,

going up on tiptoe. "And I need to wear my hair down or something," she added, yanking out the clip that held back. She fluffed out the ends with her fingers.

"What do you think?" she asked, though she could already tell from her grandmother's surprised and admiring expression that the dress was a hit.

"Wow...just plain wow," a deep voice answered in an awestruck tone.

Stephanie spun around to find Matt standing in the doorway, a suitcase in one hand and his briefcase hanging from the other. He looked tired, rumpled and badly in need of a shave, but Stephanie thought he'd never looked so good. She'd missed him so much the past few days, the feelings rose up like a giant wave inside of her. It was all she could do not to run to him and fling her arms around his neck.

"Oh...hello, Matt," she managed in careful tones. She stood back, feeling self-conscious in her fancy dress. Especially the way he was looking at her. As if she was a freshly baked pastry on a dessert cart.

"Stephanie's giving me a little fashion show," Nana explained.

"So I see," he said, stepping closer.

"It's for her sister Angie's wedding. She's some knockout, isn't she?" Bella added proudly.

Stephanie's mouth hung open, but before she could jump into the conversation, Matt spoke first.

"She certainly is. Simply stunning."

"Runs in the family," Bella noted. "You should have seen me in my younger days. My father used to chase the boys off the porch with a broom...."

Stephanie noisily cleared her throat, fearing what family legend might come out of Nana's mouth next.

Matt's gentle smile and interested look were far too encouraging.

"Nana, please, I'm sure Matt has to get into his office and check his messages. And we have to go. I'm just going to put my clothes back on. I'll be right back."

"Okay, sweetie. I'll wait right here."

Stephanie dashed into the bathroom, praying that Matt would take the cue and go. As she carefully removed the new dress, she tried to hear the conversation outside. Was he bidding her grandmother good-night…she hoped?

"That dress is something," her grandmother said. "Cost a fortune, too. Too bad she's got no date to show her off. Can you believe that?" she heard Nana say.

Stephanie's mouth dropped open. She was about to run out and put her hand over Nana's mouth when she realized that she was only wearing her underwear.

She quickly scrambled for the rest of her clothes, trying to hear Matt's reply.

"I do find that hard to believe, Bella," he said.

"Not only that…" Nana's voice got lower now and Stephanie strained to hear as she yanked up the zipper on her skirt. It jammed midway and she bit on her lip to keep from screaming. "…I hear her ex-fiancé, Tommy Torrelli, is going to show off his new girlfriend. Just to make my poor Stephanie feel bad. Does that take the cake or what? Of course, she's well rid of that guy…."

Nana, no! Why did you have to tell him that? Stephanie wanted to scream but bit down on her lip instead, hastily buttoning her blouse.

She burst through the bathroom door like a superhero,

and realized she must have looked half-crazed from the puzzled expressions on both Nana and Matt's faces.

"Just let me get my things together, Nana, and we can go," Stephanie said through gritted teeth.

She ran over to her desk and stared around, unable to remember what she needed to bring home.

Nana rose from her chair and picked up her purse. "You take your time, honey. I'm going to wait down in the lobby. I could watch the visitors desk a few minutes and learn a few things."

Now Nana was going to leave her alone with Matt. That was nearly as bad as broadcasting she couldn't find a date for Angie's wedding and was going to be publicly humiliated by her ex-fiancé.

"You don't have to go, Nana. I'll only be a minute," Stephanie insisted. She looked down and realized she'd forgotten to put on her shoes. "Oh darn, my shoes. Just a sec. I'll be right back," she mumbled. Dashing back into the bathroom, she found the right shoe quickly, but for the life of her, couldn't locate the left.

"You finish up your work and all. Don't rush."

"I had my first day of training for guest services," Stephanie heard her say to Matt in a proud tone.

"I noticed the uniform. How did it go?" Stephanie could hear the smile in his words, and pictured it in her mind's eye.

"Great. I don't mean to brag. But I caught on pretty quick."

"I'll just bet you did, Bella. I'd say you're a natural."

"I hope so…and thanks again for the opportunity," Nana said solemnly. "Will you tell Stephanie I'm waiting downstairs, but not to rush?"

"I'll do that, Bella…and you're very welcome. I

wish you luck with the new job, though I don't think you'll need it," she heard Matt say.

Stephanie finally located her left shoe wedged behind the commode, where she had kicked it off. She slipped it on in a hopping step and raced to get outside again before Nana disappeared. She just didn't want to be left alone with Matt right now. Though clearly, that was Nana's not-so-secret plan.

Out in her office again, she quickly scanned the room. Too late. Nana had flown the coop.

"She's waiting for you down in the lobby," Matt said, answering Stephanie's unspoken question.

"Yes, well…she could have waited right here. I'm ready to go." She suddenly realized a handful of her skirt was stuck in the waistband of her panty hose. She yanked it down, trying not to be too obvious.

Matt politely looked away, though she saw him hide a smile. "I thought we should take a minute and go over a few things. I have been away for a while. I want to catch up."

Stephanie walked behind her desk. "Everything has been very quiet. Very routine. There's really nothing to report."

Matt dropped into one of the armchairs across from her desk. He leaned deep into the cushions and stretched out his long lean legs, looking as if he wasn't about to be brushed off quite so easily.

"That's good. I had a chance to look over those resumés you gave me."

She felt a sudden, surprising jab in her chest that nearly took her breath away. As much as she'd wanted him to pick her replacement, hearing him talk about it made it too real.

"Any possibilities?"

"I'm not sure. There might be a few…. Is there any possibility that you'd stay?"

His tone was low and controlled, with a depth of feeling that muddled her thinking.

Stephanie took a deep breath, forcing herself not to look at him. "No, none at all. I thought we already settled this, Matt. It's not really fair to keep bringing it up again."

"Why isn't it fair? Unless you have some second thoughts. I think you do," he insisted.

Stephanie didn't answer. Of course she had second thoughts. Second, third and nine-million-and-twenty-third thoughts about it. But that didn't change things. She'd jumped into bed with him, she'd totally compromised herself and she couldn't continue to work as his assistant.

When she didn't answer, he stood up and faced her. "I missed you the last few days, Stephanie. Did you miss me?"

His admission caught her totally off guard; her breath caught in her throat and she stared at him. Her heart's honest answer hovered on her lips, though she'd dared not say the words out loud.

"I think you did," he answered for her in that same warm, low tone. "I could see it in your eyes, when you saw me in the doorway."

"You just surprised me, that's all."

He laughed lightly. "That makes two of us. You knocked me off my feet in that dress."

"Uh…thanks," she said awkwardly. Secretly, she felt a sexy glow, an unfamiliar power. If she'd ever guessed that Matt would see her in that dress and would voice that reaction, she would have willingly paid ten times the price tag.

"I agree with your grandmother. A woman wearing a dress like that needs an escort. If only to protect her from all the unwanted male attention."

"Maybe I should hire a bodyguard. One who likes Italian food and can dance the Tarantella."

"I like Italian food." He met her gaze, an eager expression softening his rugged features. Once again, Stephanie was caught off guard, and couldn't think of a clever comeback.

"And I'm a pretty good dancer," he added.

Her mouth went dry. From the moves she'd seen so far, she didn't doubt it.

What was going on? Was he lobbying to be her date for the wedding? Stephanie felt dizzy. This couldn't be possible. She must have missed something here....

"Here's a deal for you," he said suddenly.

"A deal?" What was he trying to pull now?

"If you really want to leave on Friday, I'll accept your decision, no questions asked. You pick your own replacement. I trust your judgment entirely."

He paused, tilting his head to one side as he watched her expression. His eyes looked like dark, deep, warm pools and she felt herself nearly hypnotized. Ready to agree to...anything.

She took a breath and looked away. "And...? What do you get in return for all this...compliance?"

She held her breath waiting to hear his answer.

"I take you to the wedding. It's as simple as that."

How could he dare call that simple? No offer was ever as complicated, fraught with pitfalls and snares. The idea was preposterous. But delicious to contemplate.

No, she couldn't even think of it. Not for even a nanosecond.

Stephanie shook her head. "You can't take me to the wedding. That's just…impossible."

"Why is it impossible?" He leaned across the desk, his head tilted down to catch her eye. "Are you embarrassed to be seen with me? Would I embarrass you in some way?"

"Of course not," she replied.

"I know, I know…." He stepped back and waved his hands at her. "I'm being too nice again. And you really don't like that.

Maybe I should put it a different way. Maybe I should insist, as your employer. If you don't agree, maybe I won't give you a good recommendation for your next job."

Stephanie gasped. "You wouldn't dare!"

He leaned back and appraised her. "Oh…I don't know. I might seem *nice* lately. But I can always slip back into one of my ogre-ish, inconsiderate moods."

Stephanie stared him down. "You're not serious."

"Try me."

He shrugged and smiled slightly, a deep crease dimpling one cheek. The thick five-o'clock shadow on his cheeks and jaw that would have looked scruffy on some other men made him look even more sexy and irresistible.

She realized she was staring at him too long and pulled her gaze away.

"Believe me, you really don't want to go to this wedding. You'll be bored to tears. It's nothing fancy. Just a big, noisy Italian wedding in a catering hall in Brooklyn."

"Sounds delightful. Like an art film."

"That's exactly what it is. My Sister's Big Fat Italian Wedding. It's not nearly as fun being part of the cast as you think." She could see from his expression he was not at all convinced. She knew she had to try a different tack. "Say what you want, Matt. I'm not giving in to this...blackmail."

"Don't think of it as blackmail, Stephanie. It's more of a negotiation. Now, what time should I pick you up?"

"You're acting...insane."

He smiled. "Possibly. All the more reason to humor me, I'd think."

She let out a long, frustrated breath, then turned to stare out the window, her hands on her hips. If she kept looking at him long enough, she'd not only agree to him taking her to the wedding, but she'd also soon be making love with him again on the desk.

"Stephanie, why won't you let me do this for you? Why won't you let me help you?" he asked quietly. Still, she didn't turn around or answer.

"Just this one date. I'll never bother you again," he added emphatically.

Stephanie sighed. The word *never* had such a final sound to it. After Friday, she would see very little to none of him, even if she remained at this hotel. The last few days had been just a preview of the ache she'd feel at his absence from her life.

Go for it, Stephanie, a little voice prodded. Let him take you to the wedding. You can't pass up this chance. You'll live to regret it the rest of your born days.

Finally, she turned around and looked at him. He'd gotten up from the chair and was standing just behind her. "Yes. I'll go with you to the wedding." She took a deep breath, her head bowed. "Thank you for offering."

"The pleasure will be all mine." The tone of his voice drew her head up again. She met his gaze and felt herself smile, seeing the warm light in his eyes.

She was suddenly glad and even relieved she'd given in. Suddenly elated as the reality sank in. He was going to take her to Angie's wedding. A fantasy come true. He'd look so good in a tux, her gossiping relatives would probably be shocked speechless.

For a few seconds, at least.

He stepped forward and rested his hands on her shoulders. He stared into her eyes. "We're going to have a great time," he promised her. "It's going to be a great day."

Yes, it would be. Certainly one to remember.

Stephanie smiled up at him, feeling suddenly positively buoyant. Who cared what the rest of the world thought? She'd never felt this way about anyone and she wouldn't deny herself this one harmless pleasure.

Their gaze locked and she wasn't at all surprised when he leaned forward, pulling her closer for a kiss. She was surprised that she didn't protest or argue or even try to pull away. She wrapped her arms around him, relishing the warm, hard line of his body next to hers, the hot pressure as his mouth covered her own. She felt suddenly so eager for his touch, as if the days that he'd been gone had created a deep, gnawing emptiness, a hunger only his nearness could satisfy.

Matt moaned against her mouth, and their kiss deepened. His tongue swirled against hers in an intimate dance of desire, his hands caressing her back and hips, cupping her bottom so that she felt herself lifted up against him, hip to hip. She clung to his broad shoulders, feeling herself washed away in a sea of desire. There was no mistaking his body's passionate response. Or her own as a core of molten heat grew steadily inside her.

If she didn't watch out, she'd be making love to him right on her desk in a minute, a little voice warned.

The door is closed, everyone is gone for the day. No one will ever know, another voice answered.

Stephanie.... You wouldn't dare! the first voice argued back.

But Matt was the first to pull away. Tearing his mouth from hers, he rained small, sweet kisses over her face and down the warm, smooth curve of her neck, nestling his dark head in the crook of her shoulder and hugging her close.

"What do you do to me, Stephanie? I just sort of lose my mind...." His voice was ragged, sounding half amused and half amazed.

He sighed and she did, too. He loosened his hold and gazed down at her, then smoothed back her hair from her cheek with his hand. "I tried to stay away the last few days. I thought it would be easier. But I had to come back. I missed you too much," he added quietly.

Stephanie felt almost dizzy, hearing his confession. What was he trying to tell her? She filed it away in a very private place, to think about later. Her heart pounded as she gazed up at him.

"I missed you, too," she said honestly.

She saw a spark in his dark eyes ignite and felt a secret thrill. Her admission had pleased him but before he could draw her close into another kiss, she forced herself to step out of his embrace.

"I'd better go now, Matt. My grandmother's still

waiting downstairs. She'll wonder what's happened to me."

Matt stepped back and smiled, a sexy, knowing grin. He took a handkerchief out of his pocket and wiped Stephanie's lipstick off his mouth.

"Don't worry, I think your grandmother will know perfectly well what's happened," he assured her. "I think we played right into her hands."

Stephanie couldn't argue with him. She had the same suspicions. "She's very clever. Don't underestimate her."

"I'm just figuring that out," he said with a soft laugh. "You can't underestimate any of these Rossi women."

As he held the door open, she walked out and he followed. They said good-night again in the corridor, another long, yearning gaze that left Stephanie's knees weak as she punched the button for the elevator.

Stephanie stepped inside. The doors closed on Matt's image, as he waited, watching her. Stephanie clutched her briefcase in one hand and her shopping bag in the other. She felt her head spin.

She'd taken a momentous step tonight, agreeing to let Matt be her date for the wedding. She'd come this far and she couldn't go back now. But she wasn't quite sure if the cure was worse than the disease.

Chapter Eleven

"Next time it's my turn," Nana piped up, holding up her captured bouquet as proof. "But probably hers right after that," she amended, smiling slyly at Stephanie and then Matt.

It seemed that somewhere between the rehearsal dinner and Angie's big day, her parents and grandmother had negotiated a truce. Nana had clarified that all the issues had not been worked out quite yet, but at least they were on speaking terms. In order to have a serious talk and also, to visit with her friends in the neighborhood, Nana Bella had agreed to spend the rest of the weekend in Carroll Gardens.

Stephanie kissed her cheek to say good-night. "Good luck," she whispered in Nana's ear.

"Don't worry, if things get a little rough, I still have my key to your place," Nana assured her.

Stephanie winked at her. "Give me a call tomorrow, Nana. I want to hear what happens."

Finally, she and Matt were alone, seated close together in the back of the limo. The window between their seats and the driver was closed and so was the curtain, affording them complete privacy.

Stephanie yawned and kicked off her shoes. "I'm sorry...these shoes are killing me."

Matt laughed and slid closer. "I don't mind at all. In fact, I'm going to join you." He kicked off his shoes and loosened his tie. Then he stretched out his long legs and wiggled his toes.

"I think a few of your relatives mistook me for a grape during the circle dance. I was nearly stomped to death out there."

"Brave soul that you are. I should have warned you. You can't fool around with professionals."

"Now she tells me." He sighed and smiled at her. With his tie hanging loose around his neck, his hair mussed and a faint five-o'clock shadow, he was looking awfully enticing, she thought. Better than the sweets at the dessert hour.

"How about a foot massage?" he said, and before she could answer, he lifted both her legs and placed them across his lap. Then he took hold of one of her feet and enclosed it in his large warm hands.

Stephanie was about to protest, but whatever he was doing took immediate effect, and when she opened her mouth to tell him to stop, all she could say was, "Ahhhh...gosh...that feels...good."

The corner of his mouth lifted in a half smile. "The Chinese believe the foot holds nerve points connected to the entire body."

Stephanie felt her back sink into the seat cushions. She didn't know about her entire body, but certain crucial locations were beginning to respond in most surprising ways.

His hands moved up to her ankle and then her calf, massaging the knotted muscle in soft hypnotizing circles. One hand slid up to the delicate spot at the back of her knee and then, just a few inches up her inner thigh, stroking up and down and back again until all she could do was let out a long, languorous sigh. All the food, drink and socializing had worn down her defenses. She knew she should tell him to stop, but all she really wanted to do was lie back…and enjoy the ride.

Suddenly he did stop, but just as her eyes fluttered open, he shifted closer, wrapping his arms around her shoulders so that he was cradling her across his lap. When she opened her eyes, his face was close to hers. His head dipped down and their lips met in a long, sweet, soulful kiss that seemed to go on and on. Stephanie wrapped her arms around his shoulders and stroked his face with her hands.

"I've been wanting to kiss you for hours," he confessed. "It's been a kind of sweet torture being close to you all night and not being able to touch you like this."

She'd felt the same, but was too overwhelmed to speak.

Then his dark head dipped towards hers and his hand lifted her chin. Stephanie thought to pull away, to make some reasonable protest, but all she could do was lift her hands and press them against his chest. The feeling of his firm muscles through the crisp fabric of his shirt totally disarmed her, shutting down her powers of reasoning completely.

As his mouth explored hers, his hands moved up and down her body, skimming along the curve of her narrow waist and flare of her hips, sweeping up again to cup her full breasts. She sighed, arching herself into his touch. It was as much a sign of pure frustration with herself as a sign of her surrender. It was all the encouragement Matt needed and in a heartbeat, she felt herself surrounded by his hard embrace, overwhelmed by the seeking, seductive touch of his hands and lips.

Despite all rational and moral objections Stephanie might have voiced in saner moments to kissing a man in the back of a limousine, especially this man, she found herself swept away by the moment, giving herself over to the wave of sensual pleasure that suddenly crashed over her, body and soul.

Her arms moved up, to circle his shoulders, her fingertips toying with the thick, damp strands of his hair. His mouth glided over hers, coaxing, tasting and teasing until she couldn't help but respond. She moaned quietly, in the back of her throat and the small sound inspired him with a new surge of ardor.

Finally, when it felt as if she just couldn't take any more, he pulled his head away, his breath ragged. "Stephanie…I don't know what you do to me. You know how much I want you…." He swallowed hard and stroked her cheek with the back of his hand. "But if you don't want to spend the night together…that's all right. I'll understand. When I asked to take you to the wedding, that's all I was asking about." His tone was soft and serious. "Everything else is up to you."

Stephanie couldn't answer. All she could do was gaze up at him, studying the hard lines of his too-handsome face, his large, dark eyes, his wide, soft mouth….

She felt her defenses melting, and felt herself sinking helplessly again, into the warm erotic quicksand that seemed to appear every time she let herself get this close to him.

She'd promised herself this wouldn't happen again. He'd sideswiped her into bed the first time, but this time, she'd be smarter, cooler, more self-disciplined. She would be able to share a simple kiss, maybe. Then walk away.

Who was she kidding?

Only herself, she realized.

She'd finally let her hair down and flaunted her looks at Angie's wedding. Maybe it was time to let her spirit do the same. Did she really want to leave Matt tonight and never see him again? The very thought tore her heart in two.

Maybe he wasn't the "regular guy" who would meet her at the altar in St. Anthony's Church and vow to love her loyally for the rest of his days. But maybe that wasn't what she needed right now. Or wanted. It would never be more than a short-term affair. She had no illusions about that. But it would be the passionate adventure of a lifetime, the one she'd secretly savor in her old age…once she settled down with Mr. Regular.

He hovered above her, waiting breathlessly for her answer. Stephanie reached up and took his face in her hands. Impulsively, she pulled him close and kissed him soundly, full on the lips. She felt first his surprise and then a surge of passion as he kissed her back.

"This is what I want," she whispered finally, her lips brushing his ear. "I want you, Matt. I want to stay close to you."

Her quiet words seem to let a dam loose. He sighed

and pulled her close, unleashing a torrent of passionate kisses. Somehow, they managed to keep most of
their clothes on as the car continued the ride to Manhattan. When they finally arrived at Stephanie's apartment, there were some quick repairs to be made. Matt
put his shoes on and buttoned up his shirt. Stephanie
sat up feeling dazed. She swept her hair back with her
hand and yanked up the top of her dress which had
dropped to immodest depths. Then she slipped on her
shawl and grabbed her handbag just as the driver came
around to open the door.

"Cinderella, you forgot something." She turned to
see Matt grinning at her, holding up her shoes.

"Oh…right." Stephanie quickly slipped them on.

Quite a modern interpretation of the fairy tale, she
thought, with the Prince coming back to spend the
night….

Well, it was her own version. A new chapter in her
own story. As the car sped away into the night, Matt
walked up beside her and took her hand. They walked
into the building without saying a word and then
upstairs to her front door. Her hands shook lightly as
she undid the locks and let them in.

She reached to a small lamp by the door and turned
on a light. Matt's hand followed and he shut it. He
came up behind her and hugged her from behind, his
arm circling her waist and pulling her close against his
hard length, his warm mouth nuzzling her bare neck.

"It's nice like this. We don't need the light."

No…they didn't, come to think of it, Stephanie
realized.

She leaned against him, savoring the touch of his hands
wandering over her, eliciting wonderful sensations.

He undid the side zipper of her dress and it dropped in a pool of fabric to the floor. She turned in his arms, feeling exposed in her strapless black bra and bikini underwear.

He threaded his hands into her hair, spreading it down across her shoulders. Then trailed a fingertip down her cheek, her jaw, the line of her throat and then into the valley of her breasts.

"God…you're so beautiful." His voice was low and ragged, the desire flaming high in his eyes.

Stephanie felt mesmerized, unable to move or even breathe as he dipped his head to explore the silky skin at the top of each breast with slow, tantalizing kisses. He unfastened her bra and tossed it aside. Though the summer night was hot and humid, she still felt a jolt as the cooler air touched her skin. But his warm mouth quickly covered the tip of one breast, circling with his tongue until Stephanie thought she would scream with pleasure. She clung to him, her fingers twining in his thick hair, her eyes squeezed shut. Electricity coursed up and down her limbs, her body aching for even greater satisfaction.

Just as she felt her weak legs might give way, he scooped her up and carried her into the bedroom. He laid her on the bed, then stepped away, quickly stripping off his clothes. Moonlight streamed through the curtains which were only half drawn, casting the room in soft, glowing shadows. Stephanie watched him, her head resting on the pillows. His body looked lean and powerful. Muscles rippled in his broad shoulders as he pulled off his shirt. His muscular chest was covered with dark hair, tapering down to his washboard-flat stomach, slim hips, and long, lean legs.

She opened her arms to him as he came to the bed and he moved into her embrace quickly, covering her bare body with hungry kisses, as if he was a starving man and she was a full-course banquet. His hands swept over her, her breasts, belly and thighs. She felt his hands skim her panties down her legs and then felt his fingers seek and find the silky hot center of her feminine desire. She sighed, arching her body against him as he soothed and stroked her passion even higher.

Kisses and touches and murmured words seemed to combine into a magic potion, making her feel wild and free. Stephanie felt herself soaring on a hot curling wave of passion, building and building inside as she'd never felt before.

Her hands swept across his chest and thighs and she answered his caresses with her own, her tongue laving his flat male nipples until he moaned against her mouth. She felt him hard against her, ready to make love, and she stroked and teased him, feeling a strange exciting power at the pleasure she could bring.

It wasn't her first time making love to a man and not even her first time loving Matt. But somehow, it all felt new. As if she'd broken through a secret door, into an undiscovered territory of unimagined passion and fulfillment.

Matt shifted to his side. He slipped a foil envelope out from under the pillow, which she hadn't even noticed. He removed the condom and slipped it on.

"I want to protect you this time," he said. "Down in Blue Cay we got a little carried away."

"Yes, we did," she recalled. She was usually so careful about those things, but that night, she wasn't thinking. Not about birth control, anyway. It might have been the same story tonight, if Matt wasn't so responsible, she realized.

He soon turned to her and pulled her close again. They kissed deeply, their arms and legs entwining in a sensuous lover's knot. Without needing to speak further, Stephanie leaned back, opening herself to him. She felt him enter her, smooth and hard, a thrilling shock. She clung to him, wrapping her legs around his waist as they rocked together, slowly at first, then building and building in momentum. She felt her body electrified, the pleasure building to unbearable white-hot heights, until finally she reached a peak. Exploding inside with a million dazzling lights, over and over again, like a giant star streaking across the night sky, trailing fire in its flight.

Matt moved against her, his body arching in a powerful surge and she felt him reach his peak almost at the very same moment. He cried out her name half in pleasure and half in wonder, then sank in a spent heap on top of her.

She stretched out her legs, holding him close, relishing the warm, relaxed weight of his body covering hers.

In the moments after, instead of feeling awash with regrets, Stephanie felt only deep contentment, deep connection. She'd never felt so secure, so desired, so protected in a man's embrace before. She'd never felt so free to reveal the depth of her own feelings.

Anything is worth this feeling, a small voice whispered. She had a sense that she had followed her bliss and experienced a passion she'd never quite known before.

It was more than just sex with a wonderful lover. More than even great sex, she knew. At least, for her it was. It was a feeling of complete surrender. A kind of honesty and intimacy she'd never known before. She'd never felt so in tune with a man, so open to him, so un-inhibited. She felt…new, and she liked the new Steph-anie, she decided. If that's all Matt could ever give her, it was a lot.

Stephanie opened her eyes slowly, her slumbering senses coaxed awake by the enticing smell of coffee. She found Matt sitting at the edge of the bed, smiling down at her.

"Good morning, gorgeous. Or should I say…good afternoon?"

He handed her down a cup of coffee and she eased herself up to sitting position and took it gratefully. Suddenly realizing she was naked, she used one hand to scoop up the sheet and cover her bare chest.

"What time is it?" she croaked between sips.

"A quarter to twelve." He smiled at her. "Don't look so guilty. I just got up a few minutes ago myself."

With a towel wrapped around his waist and his dark hair slicked back wet, Stephanie guessed he'd just taken a shower.

"I guess the wedding wore us out. All that dancing."

His eyebrows shot up and he grinned at her. "Some-thing wore us out. But I doubt it was the dancing."

Stephanie felt a faint blush warm her cheeks and concentrated on her coffee. How many times had they made love? Several…. A record breaker in her book. Though probably not in his, she amended.

Matt walked to the window and pulled open the curtain. "It's a beautiful day. Let's take a ride out to the Hamptons. We can spend the day and I'll bring you back in on Monday morning."

He wanted to take her out to his house in the

Hamptons? Stephanie was quietly surprised and totally pleased. It's not that she expected him to just run out of the apartment with some slam-bam-thank-you-ma'am act. But this invitation was more than she'd expected. If she didn't know better, she might even say it seemed as if they were starting off a real…dare she even think the word? …relationship.

No, she didn't even dare think it.

It was probably his usual invitation on Sunday morning for Saturday-night dates that had gone particularly well.

Don't try to analyze this, Stephanie. You'll never win.

"I'd love to go." Her bright tone revealed none of her questions and doubts. "I haven't been to the beach in ages."

She set the coffee cup on her nightstand and swung her legs off the bed, wrapping the sheet around her middle like a toga.

Matt walked over and stood before her, his handsome face beaming. Who needed a sunny day if I have you smiling at me like that, Stephanie wanted to say.

"Great. Pack a few things and we'll run up to the hotel and get my car."

She smiled at him. Then paused and licked her lips. "Matt…before we go, there's something I need to tell you."

"Oh?" His expression turned curious. And then wary. "Am I going to hate this?"

"I don't know…" she answered hesitantly. "It's just that on Monday, I'm not coming back to the hotel. I've arranged for my replacement, and I decided to take some time off. For a vacation," she finished nervously.

She saw his expression darken, looking confused and concerned. He didn't say anything for a long moment and she held her breath.

"So you've found someone to replace you after all."

She nodded. "His name is Richard Crawley. He's an assistant manager in finance. He's very sharp. Very eager to work with you."

"I know Richard. Yes, he is very bright. Not at your caliber of course," he added glumly.

"Thanks," she said in a near whisper.

Why did he have to make this so hard for her? Wasn't this what they'd agreed on? She just wanted to be honest with him, get everything out on the table so there'd be no misunderstanding later. Especially if they were spending the weekend together.

"That was our agreement," she reminded him. "I mean, after the wedding."

"Yes, I remember," he said impatiently. He sighed and stared out the window, his arms crossed over his chest. "How long will you be gone?"

"Two weeks." She tried for an even tone, but her voice came out in more of a squeak.

He stood staring out the window. She didn't know what to expect. Was he upset? Angry? Would he react with one of his infamous explosions?

Suddenly he turned to her. "Maybe I should take a vacation, too. What do you think?"

She shrugged. "Sure...why not."

"I mean, with you. Us. Together," he said, leaning closer. The corner of his mouth lifted in the hint of a teasing smile. "Would you like to spend some time together? A week or so, at the beach?"

Stephanie's breath caught in her throat. She was sure

that this was *not* the usual invitation extended to Saturday-night dates and finally felt singled out for special treatment.

Still, her first impulse was to ask, "Do you really think that's wise?"

After all, where could this lead. Nowhere. Weren't they only extending the agony? Her agony, particularly, she reflected wryly.

But The New Stephanie did not ask such reasonable, cautious questions. The New Stephanie went with the flow and the tide was clearly drifting toward Matt's house in East Hampton. All she had to do was pack a bag and catch the wave.

She walked up to Matt boldly, then tightened her shifting toga. She took his face in her hands and kissed him quickly on the lips. Then she stood back and smiled at his shocked reaction.

"I'd love to go away with you," she said honestly.

He laughed and pulled her close with warm affection. "That's good. I wasn't sure what I was going to do if you said no. Kidnap you, maybe."

His apprehension was touching, she thought. Though the truth of the matter was she'd go away with him anywhere. Hadn't he figured that out by now?

Since it was Sunday, they didn't find much traffic and the ride to East Hampton went by quickly. The village was lovely, just as she remembered it, with quaint-looking, pricey Main Street and the stately houses and shady tree-lined streets that led down to the ocean.

Matt's house was not at all what she'd expected. She'd pictured a lot of angles and glass. Something sleek and sterile. Modern and spare. When they finally pulled up the long gravel drive and parked before a rambling old colonial, she thought there had to be some mistake.

The house was the kind she'd always loved, a three-story classic Queen Anne with weathered cedar shake shingles, white trim and dark blue shutters on the windows. In the deep shade of a wide, wraparound porch, Adirondack chairs and ladder-back rockers invited some serious daydreaming, napping or ocean watching.

Matt jumped out of the car and grabbed their bags from their trunk. Stephanie reached into the backseat and took out a bag of groceries they'd picked up in town.

"Well…what do you think?" he asked her.

"I love it," Stephanie said honestly. "It's a beautiful house."

"Sort of a white elephant when I found it. I got it in an estate sale. The family that had owned it had let it go, so I got a good bargain."

By a bargain, he meant only a few million, she guessed.

"It still needs some work," he added, carrying their bags up the front steps, "but little by little, I'm getting there."

"Fixing up an old house like this can be fun," she said. "Or at least it looks fun when they do it on TV."

"Sure…if you have lots of time and loads of money. Oh, and don't forget great taste." He opened the front door, which had a beautiful brass knocker in the shape of a mermaid which looked like an antique, she noticed. Then he dropped the bags in the huge foyer which stretched straight back to the rear of the house and wide wooden framed French doors that framed a view of the beach and blue ocean.

"At least I have the money," he added with a smile.

"One out of three isn't bad," she said.

But a house like this needed more than money or even good taste. It needed…a family, she thought. Kids and dogs running through the rooms, piles of sneakers and butterfly nets at the back door. Someone cooking in the kitchen, which she suspected was as big as her entire apartment.

She sighed and forced a smile. She couldn't let these kinds of thoughts run away with her. She'd have a miserable time. The New Stephanie doesn't think this way, she reminded herself. But for the moment at least, it seemed they had lost the New Stephanie somewhere out on the Long Island Expressway.

They were soon down at the beach, soaking up the sun. Matt's strong hands, massaging sunblock on her back brought vivid images of their lovemaking to mind. He leaned over and kissed the back of her neck and she felt her body respond instantly.

Could she stand an entire week of this?

"Yes!…oh, yes!" a voice cried inside of her.

They swam and walked on the shoreline, then sat close together as the shadows grew longer and the glowing orange sun slipped toward the horizon. "Let's go inside," Matt whispered, his face nestled close to hers.

She knew exactly what he meant.

Up in the bedroom, in the fading light of the setting sun, they made slow, sensual love, exploring and learning the secrets of each other's bodies over and over again.

When Stephanie woke up the room was dark and Matt's side of the bed was empty. She heard sounds down in the kitchen and read the clock, half past seven.

She took a quick shower and pulled on a sundress. She brushed out her hair and was about to twist it up in its usual knot, then decided to wear it down, the way Matt seemed to like it best.

Following the sounds, she found Matt in the kitchen, as big and old-fashioned-looking as she'd pictured it. A collection of pots hung from a rack above a chopping block center island. The floor was black-and-white tile and the farm-style kitchen table was scarred oak.

Matt stood at the sink shucking corn, his polo shirt and shorts covered by a big white apron.

She smiled at the sight of him, working so hard at his domestic chore. "I didn't know you cooked."

"I don't," he called back over his shoulder. He smiled at her. "Well…only for special occasions. I thought we'd eat at home tonight. I hope you don't mind."

His casual use of the word *home* made her heart give off a tiny ping. She shunted the feeling aside. "No, of course not."

He dropped the last ear of corn into a bowl and carried it over to the center island. "I got everything at a farm stand, about a mile or so down the road from here. We're having lobster, corn, tomatoes and…some sort of pie. It's either blueberry or peach, I'm not sure."

"That sounds great. When did you do all this?"

"I ran out while you were sleeping. It didn't take long."

"Can I help?" she offered.

He looked up and smiled at her. A "gotcha" kind of grin.

"Aha! So you can cook. I knew your mother wouldn't lie to me."

Stephanie smiled, feeling caught red-handed. "You'd

be surprised at what she'll say for the sake of *marketing* one of her daughters."

He laughed and took a bottle of wine out of the refrigerator. Then, with a deft twist of his wrist, he had it instantly uncorked. He poured two glasses and handed Stephanie one.

"Here's to…our vacation." He gazed at her briefly with a soft smile. "So far, I'm having the best ever."

She smiled at him, feeling suddenly shy. "Me too," she agreed. They touched glasses and sipped the wine.

Stephanie helped fix the rest of the meal and soon they were sitting out on the back porch, sipping more wine and cracking open their steamed lobsters.

They talked about problems at the hotel, with Matt sounding out Stephanie for her advice. But they soon moved on to more personal matters. The kind of summer vacations they'd each spent with their family, for one thing. Stephanie related how her parents would pack everyone up in their station wagon, including Nana and the family pets, and charge up to a cabin in the Adirondacks. It was not exactly an idyllic, secluded mountain retreat since the neighboring cabins were rented by other family members, her aunts and uncles and cousins.

"I always thought vacations were a chance to get away…not take the whole neighborhood with you," Stephanie said with a shrug. Matt smiled at the story. He sat back and dabbed his mouth with a napkin.

"I can't really remember any family vacations," he said. "I guess maybe one time, before my mother died, my parents took my brother and me to a beach somewhere. Maine, maybe." He shrugged. "My father never spent much time with us after she was gone. Day after school closed, we were packed off to camp." He shrugged. "Camp was fun though. I didn't mind it. I enjoyed the sports, baseball mostly."

"Yes, I can see that," she said.

She had the feeling that he had minded being shipped off to camp and denied the attention of his father. He'd minded it a lot, but was just too proud—or maybe, still too hurt—to admit it. He always seemed so confident and in control. But there were many sad memories he pushed aside or covered over. Maybe that's what made him work so hard, what had driven him to such early, impressive success. But it had come at a cost, she realized.

"Listen, I never got to thank you for taking me to the wedding. I know I argued with you about it, but I really appreciated having you there, Matt. It made a world of difference to me."

He looked moved by her words. He smiled softly at her, the light from the candle on the table casting his face in soft shadows. "I enjoyed being with you there, Stephanie. You don't have to thank me. Weddings can be fun. It's nice to see a couple starting off fresh, all that true love and optimism."

She couldn't quite tell if he was being serious now…or cynical. "That part is nice," she agreed. "It's hard to tell though how many couples will stay together. Sometimes it feels as if you haven't even gotten your dress back from the cleaners before you're hearing the couple is getting a divorce."

He laughed. "I know what you mean. It's sort of a shock…but it happens. Couples just don't stay together anymore. Not like your parents, for example. I admire that."

She studied him a moment. He stared down at the

table, tracing the edge of his wineglass with his fingertip. At this uncomfortable point in the conversation, The Old Stephanie would have diplomatically changed the subject.

The New Stephanie wanted to know more. Needed to know more. She needed to know what she was up against.

Chapter Twelve

"You were married once, right?"

Matt looked up and nodded, clearly surprised at the question.

"That's right."

"Were you married very long?"

"Five years. We met in college and got married right after." His tone was curt, but still didn't put her off.

"Oh, you were young."

"Yes...young and naive," he replied, definitely sounding cynical now. "Or maybe I should just say stupid."

She took a breath, too intrigued now to quit. "You were too young to get married? Is that what you mean?"

He looked up at her briefly, the warm light missing from his dark eyes. "Too young to understand women. The games some of them play," he said bluntly. "The woman I married, Lindsay. She was beautiful, smart, everything I'd ever wanted. I really loved her and thought she loved me, too. But she'd really just wanted to marry someone rich. She trapped me, claiming she was pregnant. I really didn't want kids, but I loved her, so we got married."

The last phrase hit a silent bull's eye. He doesn't want kids, she realized. That would account somewhat for all the womanizing. He doesn't want to be tied down with a wife and family.

She felt a huge pain in her heart, her foolish hopes deflating like a busted balloon. Still, she forced herself to go on, to get the whole story. "So you got married. Then what?"

He smiled at her and she wondered if he was just going to put her off instead of answer. Finally he shrugged.

"Lindsay wanted me to go to law school and then join her father's practice in the city. I wanted a degree in business instead. I'd inherited some money from my mother and wanted to start my own company. I wasn't sure yet quite what I'd do, but this was really my dream, all I was interested in. I didn't want to study law, or anything like it.

"But Lindsay was convinced I'd fail and lose everything. I guess you could say she didn't have much faith in me. Or maybe she just couldn't stand the idea of losing all that money. When she figured out she couldn't force me to live my life the way she wanted, she called in her father's buddies and filed for a divorce.

"Somehow she managed to take away practically all my seed money for the business. So, she left me, got most of my money, and finally, told me she'd never really loved me. And guess what, she'd never even been expecting a baby. That had been a lie, too."

He reported the story in a bland, cool tone. Yet Stephanie could sense the pain and anger still rumbling beneath, like a volcano that wasn't quite sleeping. Matt lifted his wineglass and took a long sip.

"Sorry for the gruesome details. But you did ask."

"Yes, I did," she agreed. "That's a sad story."

He shrugged. "It's almost ten years. I've recovered. She's married again, a lawyer I hear. Surprise, surprise. So everyone's happy."

He forced a smile. Stephanie met his glance, but didn't smile back. She didn't think he was happy. Not deep down inside, where it really counted. She didn't think he still loved his ex-wife. Far from it. But he'd never forgiven her and that was just as much a hurdle for any woman trying to get close to him.

"Ready for dessert? I still have that mystery pie," he coaxed her.

"I'm pretty full. How about a walk on the beach first?" she suggested.

His expression brightened. "Great idea. It's a perfect night for a walk."

They walked off the porch together and he took her hand as they followed the stone path that led to the beach. As they walked toward the water, Matt slung his arm around her shoulder and she put her arm around his waist. They walked along the shoreline in a comfortable step, as if they'd been together for years, she thought.

They didn't talk at all, but it was an easy, relaxed silence. The sky was clear, a deep dark blue studded with stars, and the ocean looked almost black. The waves tumbled into the shoreline and the soft foam swallowed their footprints on the sand.

Suddenly Matt turned toward her. He smoothed some blowing strands of hair off her cheek and kissed her, a sweet, affectionate kiss that made her feel happy inside.

"What was that for?" she asked him with a smile.

He shrugged. "I just like having you here."

She tilted her head to one side and squinted her eyes at him. "You don't have any lack of houseguests. From what I hear." She could see him trying valiantly to suppress a wolfish grin.

"True…but maybe not as many as you might think. Besides, you can be in the middle of a crowd and still feel lonely."

That was true enough. Towards the end of her relationship with Tommy, she'd felt very lonely when they were together. They just didn't seem to connect.

She did feel connected to Matt. In a deep, essential, almost mysterious way. Sometimes she felt as if she'd always known him. Or had an intuition of him, deep in her soul.

She took his hand and they headed back down the beach toward his house again. She had other intuitions, too. Some that were more like warning bells sounding. But Stephanie knew she was already in too deep to turn and run away.

The sunny days and clear summer nights at Matt's house passed quickly, falling one into the next like flower petals on a pond. They walked on the beach, morning and night, swam and sunbathed, rode bikes and even a few horses. They played tennis and miniature golf. Ate at posh restaurants and cooked barbecues.

They window-shopped in the wealthy, staid village and browsed the antique barns and farm stands.

They made love whenever the mood struck—morning, noon and night. On the beach, in the pool, in the shower, and in the garden, curtained by a willow tree. One rare, rainy afternoon, in the library in front of a fire, and one bright morning, on the kitchen table.

Matt was tender and passionate, even loving. But Stephanie did not fool herself into believing that he was in love with her. Though she felt sure that she had fallen in love with him.

Looking back, she couldn't tell when it had happened. Maybe the first time they'd made love, back on Blue Cay. Or even the first time their eyes had met.

She did know that her feelings were real and irrevocable. Though there seemed little hope of a lasting commitment, she willed herself to enjoy their time together, however long it lasted.

They spent nearly every minute of each day together, with Matt slipping off to his home office for an hour or so each day to check in with the hotel. Richard Crawley seemed to be doing very well, running the entire place without a hitch. They both laughed about Matt's dispensability.

Overall though, Matt didn't talk much about work, and handled even the troublesome reports with a mellow, detached air. A jolting difference from the Type A, hands-on, semi-control freak she'd been working for, Stephanie reflected. She wondered what had caused the change. Maybe the sea air?

Stephanie adopted the same attitude to her distractions that intruded on their private world—namely her family, who had been in a mild uproar ever since Nana Bella's return.

Talking with her son and daughter-in-law, Nana had put forth certain conditions; her own apartment, freedom to come and go as she pleased, and continuing with her job at the hotel.

Dominic was unwilling to bend on any of his mother's points. He didn't think Nana needed to live alone. That's why he'd encouraged her to sell her house and he thought she was too old to work and endanger her health. As for coming and going, the world was a dangerous place, he believed. "It isn't the 1940s anymore," he bellowed. "A woman her age can't just go wandering around. Anything can happen... God forbid."

Something would happen, Stephanie feared. Nana was going to leave home again. It seemed just a matter of time. Nana, her parents and even her sisters called daily, reporting both sides of the story. They only knew she was on vacation at a beach house on Long Island with a friend. She had carefully given the impression that the friend was another woman and nobody seemed to guess it was Matt.

Though they carefully avoided talking about it, Matt and Stephanie both knew their days in paradise were numbered. Matt could manage only so long running the company long-distance, and Stephanie also felt pressure to return to the real world and sort out her life. Would she go back to her old job in the hotel in the operations department? Would she ask for a transfer or even apply for a job at some other chain? She thought that time out of the city would help her sort out the question, but it all seemed even more confusing, now that she'd fallen so hard and fast for Matt.

On Saturday night, Matt took her out to a special restaurant. The place was hard to find, nestled in a secluded spot on the waterfront in a distant town, but Matt claimed it was well worth the ride. From the outside, it looked like an old barge. But within, it was very elegant, with soft lighting, pale peach walls, golden trim and polished wooden moldings. The tables were set with rich linen cloths, fine china and shimmering crystal.

The maître d' greeted Matt by name and brought them right to a table. The best in the house, Stephanie thought.

Matt ordered champagne and they drank from tall fluted glasses and gazed out at the water view. He set his glass down and smiled at her with a curious look. "You put your hair up tonight," he said.

Stephanie self-consciously touched the smooth knot of hair gathered at her nape. "I just wanted to get it out of the way."

"I'm just surprised. I haven't seen it like that for awhile. It reminds me of the first time I saw you…I was thinking, God, that woman is beautiful. She has a face from a Renaissance painting."

For all their intimacy the past week, his compliments still had the power to make her blush.

"Thank you," she said quietly. "That's very…sweet."

He smiled at her, his dark eyes flashing. "I didn't say it to be sweet. It's just true. Have you ever been to Florence? I think you'd love it. There's some of the most wonderful art in the world there."

Stephanie shook her head. Putting herself through school, then building her career and paying back student loans had kept her busy the past years. She loved to travel but so far had neither the time nor the extra money to do it.

"No, I haven't been to Italy yet. I'd love to go though."

He reached over and took her hand. "I'd love to take you there."

Stephanie didn't know how to reply. The look in his eyes seemed so sincere and promised so much. But perhaps he made these kinds of remarks to every woman he dated. Of which there were many, she sadly reflected. What would Monday in the real world bring? Would this passionate fling even stand the test of returning to the city? His track record wasn't very promising.

Matt held up his glass for a toast. "To our next vacation?"

Stephanie forced a smile and touched her glass to his. The crystal rang, a bright sound that seemed to scatter her worries and bode a bright future for them.

As the dinner continued, Stephanie felt herself relax. She stopped worrying about the future and focused only on Matt's conversation and company. As usual, they had no lack of interesting things to talk about but could also sit without talking, feeling in perfect harmony.

Stephanie was contentedly eating her dessert, a delectable chocolate soufflé, when she suddenly noticed a gift box at her place, slipped onto the table right under her nose.

She stared at the box, afraid to touch it.

"That's for you…in case you didn't guess," Matt said in a wry tone.

"Why did you get me a gift? You didn't have to do that," she protested.

"I just wanted to buy you something. You're not very

good at accepting gifts, are you?" he teased her. "I should have known. Go ahead. Open it."

She glanced at him, then pulled the ribbon loose. She opened the box to find a sparkling diamond-and-sapphire bracelet. She felt a lump in her throat and swallowed hard. It had to be worth a small fortune. The distinctive blue box came from a world-famous jeweler. The main store was on Fifth Avenue but she knew there was also a store in town. She'd probably never even touched a piece of jewelry worth this much.

"If it doesn't please you, you can exchange it. We'll pick out something else," he said, obviously wondering why she didn't touch it.

"I love it. It's...fantastic," Stephanie answered, looking up at him. "But I'm not sure...."

He looked confused. "What aren't you sure about?"

She looked back at the bracelet again, briefly considering if she should keep it. It seemed such a lavish gift. It didn't seem right somehow to accept.

"It's just so...expensive," she said honestly. "I'm not sure I can accept this, Matt."

Matt looked at her a moment and softly laughed. He shook his head. "Stephanie, you have to be the most unspoiled woman I've known. Of course you can accept it. I want you to have it. Please?"

The expression on his handsome, beloved face was finally her undoing. She could see now it was a gift from the heart and that was the real value of it to her.

She glanced at him. "Yes...and thank you. Thank you very much."

She picked up the bracelet and draped it over her wrist. Matt leaned over quickly and fastened the clasp. She held out her arm and admired it. The jewels glittered like stars plucked from the sky, even in the low light.

"It's beautiful. I'll cherish it, always." She smiled shyly. "And you're right. I'm not very good at accepting presents. Especially an outrageous one, like this."

"We'll have to work on that," he said with a slow smile.

He slipped his arm around her shoulder and pulled her close to place a deep warm kiss on her lips.

"Are you happy?" he asked quietly.

She nodded. "Yes, very."

He gazed into her eyes. "Good...then so am I."

He kissed her again and Stephanie felt all her worries melt away, like the puddle of abandoned soufflé at the bottom of her dish.

When they returned to Matt's house, Stephanie checked the messages on her cell phone. There were two numbers, both familiar—Nana and her parents.

"Any calls?" Matt teased her. He already knew the answer.

"Just the usual suspects. I'd better check though and see what's going on," Stephanie replied in a weary voice.

The first message was from Nana. "I just want you to know that things didn't work out. Your father and I had it out again and he's as pigheaded as ever. I'm moving back to your place. Just for a little while. I hope it's okay."

Oh dear. She'd expected as much. The next was from her mother. "Stephanie, it's me. Some bad news, honey. Your father was having chest pains tonight, so I took him into the hospital. First Presbyterian in Park Slope. The doctor is going to do some tests. Your sisters are with me and everything is okay so far. I just wanted you to know what's going on."

Dominic was resting comfortably, her mother reported,

but the doctors still couldn't say if he'd had a heart attack. "Okay, honey. Don't worry. Call me when you can."

When she finally looked up from the phone, Matt was staring at her. "Is something wrong?"

"My grandmother is hiding out in my apartment again and my father is in the hospital. Chest pains, but they're not sure if he's had a heart attack."

Matt's expression darkened with concern. "You should be with your family now. They need you. Let's get our things together and I'll take you back to the city right away."

Stephanie felt so grateful for the way he'd instantly understood and she didn't have to explain it to him. "Yes, I'd better go. I'm sorry to cut the week short."

"Don't be ridiculous. This is an emergency."

He put his arms around her and hugged her close. "Are you worried about your dad?" he asked quietly.

His comforting touch caught her off guard. It was always Stephanie's way to show a calm, controlled persona, even in a crisis. Especially in a crisis. But once he held her close, she felt her mask crumble.

Chapter Thirteen

"Yes…a little," she admitted. Her voice was suddenly trembling. She didn't want to cry but felt her eyes fill with tears.

"He'll be okay, don't worry," Matt whispered. "He got to the hospital quickly and they're figuring it out. That's the important thing."

She nodded against his shoulder, unable to answer. "He's getting some tests right now. Maybe by the time we get there they'll know something."

"Yes, I hope they do." He hugged her again, then let her go. "It's not late. We can be there by midnight."

"I'll call my mother back and let her know I'm on my way," Stephanie said.

Her mother was very grateful to hear she was coming and said she would wait at the hospital with

Stephanie's father, since they still didn't know what was wrong with him.

"I'm fine, honey. Don't you worry," her father told her. "Just a little indigestion. You know how it gets me."

Stephanie doubted it was only indigestion. But he did sound strong. Still, she was eager to see both of them. She was eager to be with her family.

Matt pushed the speed limit on the dark, empty highway. Saturday night seemed the perfect time to make the commute from the resort area to the city on a route that was typically bumper-to-bumper.

As Matt had predicted, it was nearly midnight when they reached the hospital in Brooklyn. They followed the signs to the Emergency Room and soon located Stephanie's father in a curtained corner of a large area full of patient beds. Stephanie pulled back the edge of a green curtain and found most of her family sitting there, packed in like six campers in a three-man tent.

Her mother was sitting in a plastic chair by her father's bed and her head popped up instantly at the sight of Stephanie.

"Stephanie…what timing. The doctor is coming by in a minute to tell us what's wrong with Daddy."

Her father shifted in his hospital bed, wearing a pale green cotton gown and a grumpy expression. He waved his hand. "There's nothing wrong with me, Fran, for goodness' sake. It's a little indigestion. It happens every time I eat sausage and peppers."

"And fight with your mother," Stephanie's mother added sharply. "Let's not forget that part."

"Where is Nana?" Stephanie asked. She looked at her sister Christine and her brother-in-law Kevin.

Neither of them answered. Gina and her husband Tom also looked away when she met their gaze.

Stephanie looked at her mother. "Didn't you tell her?"

"Well…your father didn't want to worry her. Until he knows what's what."

"You should have called her. She'll be even more worried when she hears you were sick and no one called."

Her father met her a gaze a second, then guiltily looked away. "Your nana took off again. The Little Old Lady From Pasadena—go granny, go. Who knows where she is?"

"At my apartment again. Where do you think she'd go?"

She took a breath and held her temper. It wouldn't do to start arguing with her father. He might have had a heart attack, though in truth, seeing him now she did think it was too much sausage and peppers. And the stress of haggling with her grandmother. Whatever it was, she did feel sorry for him. She walked to his bedside and gave him a kiss.

"Sorry, Dad. It will all work out with Nana. We have to worry about getting you out of here first."

Her father patted her hand. "Don't worry about me, kid. I'm strong as an ox…hey, who's that hiding behind the curtain, the Wizard of Oz or something?"

"Just me." Matt stepped forward, an amused smile brightening his face. He'd been standing behind Stephanie the whole time, but the cubicle had been so crowded he didn't have a chance to step forward and say hello.

"How are you feeling, Dominic?" Matt asked.

"I'm all right. I had a little indigestion and my wife calls 911. In the middle of a ball game besides. Cardoza was pitching too. Working on a no-hitter in the seventh inning. Can you beat that?"

"Tough break. That reminds me, I didn't forget about those tickets I promised you. There's a game at home against the Red Sox, two weeks from now. Think you can make it?"

"You bet I will. I'll drive myself over in an ambulance if I need to."

Everyone in the room laughed, including Matt, who laughed the loudest. Her father looked much better now than when she had arrived, she noticed. It was amazing what a few box seat tickets to Yankee Stadium could do.

The curtain was pulled aside and a woman in a white lab coat appeared. From her weary look and the stethoscope slung around her neck Stephanie guessed this was her father's doctor.

"Well, quite a gathering in here. Sounds like a comedy club. Hello, Mr. Rossi. I'm Dr. Krasner. I just read your tests and I wanted to go over the results with you."

Her father sat up, looking suddenly alert. "Shoot, Doc. Did I have a heart attack?"

"No, your heart is fine. No sign of a cardiac problem at all."

"Thank God." Her mother took the holy medal that was hanging around her neck on a gold chain and quickly kissed it.

"But there are other problems, Mr. Rossi. We need to talk."

"Uh-oh, that doesn't sound good." Dominic shook his head, slumping down a bit against the pillows.

"Well, it all depends on how you look at it. You have

an ulcer, sir. A nasty one. It's amazing you haven't come in for treatment before this."

"An ulcer? Me? I'm not the nervous type at all," he exclaimed.

Francesca shook her head. "Oh boy, here we go," she murmured to herself.

"Maybe we should step out a few minutes. Give you some privacy with the doctor, Dad," Christine said. She touched her husband's arm and they slipped out of the cubicle.

Stephanie turned to her mother. "I'll be right back. You and Dad talk to the doctor." Her mother nodded in answer.

Out in the corridor, Stephanie and Matt met up with her sisters and their spouses. "We're going down to the cafeteria for some coffee. Want to come?" Christine said.

"Sure…we'll catch up in a minute," Stephanie replied.

Once the group had gone, she turned to Matt. "This could drag on all night. You don't need to stay."

He shrugged. "I can stay if you want me to."

She felt torn. On one hand she did want him to stay, but on the other, she knew his continued presence would invite too much speculation from her family. How could she explain their relationship to them when she didn't even understand it herself?

She also thought she'd probably stay in Brooklyn tonight. With both Nana and Angie gone, the house was empty and her mother would need some company.

This was the real world, bursting her pleasant bubble with a resounding pop already, she thought.

"It's almost one. I think you should go home and get some sleep. Besides, I'm going back to my parents' house tonight. I think I should stay with my mom and keep her company. She hates to be in the house alone."

Matt seemed a bit surprised but his expression quickly shifted to acceptance and understanding. "Of course. She seems a bit upset. You should be with her."

Once again, Stephanie was grateful for his understanding and his kindness towards her father. He took her hand as they walked toward the exit. "Don't worry about your father. An ulcer is serious business, but if he watches his diet and takes his medication, he'll be fine in no time."

"He's stubborn when it comes to medical matters. But I think that doctor will put a scare into him," Stephanie said.

She waited by the glass entrance doors while Matt retrieved her bag from the car and brought it to her. Then they managed to find a private corner in the lobby to say good-night.

Matt looped his arms around her waist and pulled her close. "I'm going to miss you, Stephanie. We've been together every day for a week now."

She was going to miss him, too. Terribly, but it was hard for her to admit it so openly. "Once you get back at work on Monday, all those e-mails will distract you."

"Once I'm back at work, I'll miss you more," he insisted. "Richard Crawley might be a whiz…but he doesn't have your legs by a longshot."

"You chauvinist."

"Possibly. But hold your fire. I hear we're protected as an endangered species these days."

She couldn't help but smile at him. His head dipped down and he kissed her soundly, pulling her even closer and deepening their kiss as if they were entirely alone, standing in front of the doors to the deck off the big bedroom at the house in East Hampton. With her eyes squeezed shut, Stephanie could almost hear the sound of the ocean waves crashing to the shore.

No…more like the rattle and crash of a medicine cart rolling by. She sighed against his mouth and slowly pulled away.

"I'll call you," he whispered. "I want to know what's happening."

She nodded, feeling too emotional to speak. There was so much she suddenly wanted to say, but couldn't quite put it into words. "Okay," she managed. "Good night, Matt."

He cast her a thin smile. "Good night."

Then he turned and walked through the doors, out into the parking lot. Stephanie watched through the glass until she lost sight of him.

Stephanie woke the next morning in her old bedroom. She glanced around and felt depressed. It was such a radical change from waking up in Matt's arms in the big old house by the sea.

Funny how quickly you lose that vacation feeling, she quipped to herself. She heard her mother down in the kitchen and forced herself to sit up. The smell of coffee, eggs and toast awakened her appetite. Stephanie felt hungry…then suddenly, not so good at all. She rushed to the bathroom and made it just in time. Her stomach was empty so there wasn't much to lose. But the feeling was awful.

She pushed herself up and splashed her face with cold water, then brushed her teeth. She peered in the mirror, thinking she looked pale, even under her tan.

"Great, just what I need right now. A stomach bug."

She dragged herself downstairs and sat in a kitchen chair. Her mother was dressed, wearing an apron over a floral print dress. She greeted Stephanie, then finally turned around to look at her.

"Gee, you don't look so good, honey."

"I think I caught a bug. I just got sick."

"Oh boy. That's not good. I'll make you some tea and toast."

"That's okay, Mom. I can get it." Stephanie rose and put some water on to boil. The tea seemed like a good idea. In the morning she was usually a die-hard coffee fiend. She just couldn't face it today though.

She sat down again and forced a smile. "What time are we going to see Dad?"

"Visiting hours start at eleven. Your Aunt Betty and Uncle Sal are coming. I spoke to them this morning."

"That's nice."

"And Gert and Micky might come too. Your father needs company. It will cheer him up."

"Yes, definitely." Stephanie agreed.

Betty was her mother's sister. Gert and Micky were family friends. Stephanie was sure that before the day was through, half of Brooklyn would be marching over to see her father.

"So…how was your vacation?" her mother asked innocently. "You sure got a tan."

"It was great. Beautiful weather." Stephanie jumped up to fix her tea.

"Matt seemed tanned too," her mother said.

"Really…I didn't notice."

Her mother cast her a look. Stephanie knew she was dying to ask if they had been away together. But she didn't want to be so direct. Unlike her sisters, who didn't hesitate to grill her last night over coffee after he'd left.

"He's a very nice guy, giving your father tickets to the ball game like that. Very generous."

"He is generous." Stephanie poured the hot water in a mug with a tea bag and swished it around with a spoon.

"Is that a new bracelet?" her mother asked.

Stephanie looked up suddenly, then down at her wrist. "Um…yes, it is. Do you like it?"

"It's beautiful. It's amazing how real that costume jewelry looks these days, isn't it? Your sister Gina bought a ring off the shopping channel, diamond and emeralds in a little flower. Looked like the real thing to me."

Stephanie smiled at her and stirred a spoonful of sugar into her tea. "You never know, Mom," she agreed.

They talked a bit more about her father's ulcer and the problems with Nana. The first could be solved with diet and medicine. The second was not so easy to cure.

"I'll call her this morning," Stephanie told her mother. "Don't worry, I'll explain everything. I'll make sure she doesn't get Dad all worked up again."

"I hope so, Stephanie. I'd call myself, but I think at this point, you can handle her better."

Her mother had so much stress right now, Stephanie didn't mind taking over the Nana front.

"Well, I'm going to church. I can make the ten o'clock mass," her mother announced. "It eases your mind. Want to come?"

Stephanie smiled and shook her head. "Not today, Mom. You go ahead."

Her mother gazed at her. "Stephanie…I know you're an adult and you lead your own life. You're a real inde-

pendent woman, like in the magazines. But sweetheart...watch out for yourself, okay? You know how
you got so tanned last week?"

Stephanie sat up, unsure of what her mother was
getting at. "I didn't use enough sunblock?"

Her mother smiled knowingly. "You're playing with
fire, honey. I know I can't tell you what to do. But I'm
your mother. I worry anyway. You'll see when it's your
turn," she added with a sigh as she stood up from her
chair.

"*If* and when," Stephanie corrected her.

"Oh, hon. It will happen. Before you know it." She
patted Stephanie's shoulder. "I'll see you later. Go back
to bed, you look terrible."

"Thanks, Mom." Stephanie laughed and shook her
head. Trust your mother to tell you the truth. Even when
it hurts, she thought.

Stephanie stayed on in Brooklyn for the rest of the
week. She kept her mother company for a few nights
and then helped handle her father, who came home on
Wednesday. He was not a good patient under any circumstances and when he heard the list of foods he
wasn't allowed to eat anymore, Stephanie thought she
might have to call 911 again.

But finally, he came to his senses and begrudgingly
accepted his fate. There would be no more House of
Rossi red wine served at the dinner table each night, she
realized. A blessing in disguise.

Her father's emergency jolted her grandmother into
instant sympathy and remorse. She was wise enough to
see her own part in Dominic's crisis. Like a true mother,
she rushed to his hospital bed and pampered him. But
despite her concern for her son's health, she still wasn't

willing to budge on her demands. Stephanie was the only one who could make any headway with her and little by little, over the course of several days, she finally worked out a compromise.

Her parents would renovate the basement into an apartment for Nana Bella, complete with a separate entrance. She would give up her job at the hotel, since the commute seemed too long from Brooklyn for her. But she would find a part-time job someplace in the neighborhood. She didn't have to ask permission every time she wanted to step foot out of the house. But she did need to call in from her cell phone regularly.

"Happy now, Ma?" Dominic asked from his recliner in the living room.

"You're a good son, Dominic. I'm lighting a candle for you. For your stomach," Bella told him.

"Thanks, Mom. My stomach needs all the help it can get."

When Stephanie finally returned to her apartment on Saturday, she found her grandmother there, packing her things to move back to Brooklyn

"It's time I go back anyway. Your mother needs me now to take care of your father."

That was true. But Nana liked to be needed, too.

"They gave me a little going-away party at the hotel yesterday," she told Stephanie. "Wasn't that nice?"

"Very nice. You only worked there a few weeks."

"Well, they said I did a good job and I could always come back if I wanted."

"That's nice to know."

Stephanie wondered if Matt had gone to Nana Bella's party. But she didn't ask. They had spoken on the phone every day, but she hadn't seen him since Saturday night, at the hospital. Their conversations had been brief and often unsatisfying, even though Matt kept reminding her how much he missed her.

He'd offered to come out and see her several times, but she put him off. She felt distracted and over-whelmed by all the events at her parents' house. And other matters too that she wasn't ready to talk about. With anyone.

It was hard to communicate over the phone some-times. Especially when you felt so much and were so afraid to admit it.

She unpacked a few groceries and started to put them away in the kitchen. Nana stood nearby, watching her. "What's that stuff you bought in the little cups? Yogurt?'

Stephanie shook her head. "Rice pudding."

"Rice pudding?" Nana walked closer and picked up the package. "You hate rice pudding. I used to make it when you were a baby and you'd spit it right back out at me. Your sister Christine, now she loved rice pudding. With raisins," Nana recalled. "The yellow kind, not the brown ones."

Stephanie shrugged and stuck the pack of pudding into the fridge. "I don't know, I just felt like having some."

Nana pinned her with a steely-eyed stare. "Stepha-nie…you want to tell me something? I'm not like your mother, you know. I don't get shocked so easy."

Stephanie gave her grandmother an innocent look. "I don't know what you mean, Nana. What would I want to tell you?"

"Well…the only time I ever had a craving for rice pudding, I was pregnant. First with your father, and then with your two aunts. Now the way you look lately, the way you fall asleep at the six-o'clock news and get green around the gills when you smell something cooking…well, that makes an old lady like me think you might have something you want to talk about."

Stephanie stared at her grandmother for a long moment. She willed herself to stay calm and not give herself away. But she couldn't help it. She soon broke down, nodding her head and feeling her eyes fill with tears.

"It's true, Nana. I'm…expecting a baby."

Nana beamed. "That's wonderful! God bless!"

She leaned over and gave Stephanie a huge hug and a kiss.

"Nana, how could you say that? It's a total disaster."

"Does Matthew know?" Nana asked boldly.

Stephanie blinked and sighed. "No…he doesn't. I just figured it out myself the other day. I've had no chance to tell him."

"Well, what are you waiting for? Call him, have him come right over. He needs to hear the happy news."

Stephanie swallowed hard, fighting hard to compose herself. To her the news was not entirely happy. And it wouldn't be to Matthew either, she had no illusions about that.

"It's not that simple, Nana. It's not simple at all…I don't know what to do."

Nana looked shocked and confused. She sighed and forced a smile. "You young people. You make everything so complicated. You love him, he loves you. He'll love the baby, too. Don't worry."

But that's just what she was worried about. "Nana…you don't understand. Matt and I…well, it's not like that. He cares for me. He's a good man, a good person. But he doesn't want a wife and a family. He's just not that type."

Nana gave her a long look. "*Bella,* you have to tell him. It's his baby, too."

Stephanie met her loving gaze, then looked away. "Yes…you're right. I'll tell him soon. As soon as I can," she promised.

Nana nodded. "Very good…now, you go in the living room and put your feet up. Have a nice rest." She pulled an apron from a hook and wrapped it around her middle. "I'm going to make you some nice, *homemade* rice pudding. You can't eat that stuff in the plastic cup. It's full of chemicals. It's not good for the baby," she said very seriously.

Stephanie smiled and kissed her cheek. She didn't have the will or the strength to argue.

After a nap and a bowl of Nana's fortifying pudding, Stephanie summoned up the nerve to call Matt. He sounded very happy to hear her voice and she felt a boost of courage.

They arranged to have dinner that night at a nearby restaurant and Matt insisted on coming to her apartment to pick her up.

"I can't wait to see you," Matt said in a husky voice. "I've been dreaming of you every night…but it doesn't come close to the real thing."

Stephanie sighed. She wished with all her heart they could have one more blissful night together before she told him her secret. But that wouldn't be fair, she realized.

Though once he heard the truth, there was a good chance they would never be together that way again.

Matt wasn't going to take this well, she thought. He'd told her point-blank he didn't want children. He might even think she was trying to trap him into marriage, like his ex-wife.

She touched her stomach, which was still flat as a pancake. Despite all her worries, she was truly thrilled to be pregnant, to know a child, hers and Matt's, was growing inside of her. It was the thrill of a lifetime and no matter what happened, at least she had her baby to look forward to now.

Her family had always considered her the liberated one, so being a single mother shouldn't be that big a jump for them, she consoled herself. Though her parents would go through their usual theatrics—especially her father. At least he had some heavy duty medication for his stomach now.

Stephanie worked hard on her hair and makeup. She wasn't at her best this week but wanted to look nice for Matt. She chose a long flowered skirt and a sleeveless peach silk top with a soft, draped neckline.

She wore her hair long and loose around her shoulders, the way Matt seemed to like it best. She glanced at herself in the mirror and thought she looked pretty good…under the circumstances. She decided to keep the lights low in the living room and add a few candles.

She felt butterflies in her stomach. Almost as if it was a first date. She dreaded telling Matt the real reason she'd asked him to see her tonight.

But she knew that Nana was right. She had to tell him. He had a right to know.

Matt rang the doorbell at precisely eight, just as they had planned. She buzzed him up and ran to the front door. She had it opened before he even knocked.

There was no avoiding it any longer.

Chapter Fourteen

Matt stood in the doorway. He didn't say a word, just met her gaze, smiling faintly.

Then he slammed the door behind him and pulled her close, capturing her mouth in a long, deep kiss. Stephanie melted into his arms, instantly losing all defenses.

She had missed him so much, yearned for his touch, the feeling of his body next to her own, the smell of his hair and skin. The thrilling sound of his voice, calling her name.

"God...I missed you..." he murmured between hungry kisses.

They moved from the front door, into the living room. Matt gently tugged her down on the couch and she clung to him, not even pausing in their kiss as she stretched out alongside him on the cushions. She felt his hands slip off her blouse as she was busily tugging his shirt free from the waist of his pants and unfastening the catch above the zipper.

"Let's go in the bedroom," he whispered. "This couch is too lumpy…."

Stephanie nodded in agreement, then slowly came to her senses as she started to sit up.

"Wait…." She took a deep breath. She touched her hand to her forehead. "I need to talk to you about something, Matt."

She glanced at him. He looked confused. "Right now?" His hair was mussed and his shirt undone, his eyes glazed with desire.

"Yes…I'm sorry. It's important." She sighed and pulled away, then slipped her top on again.

"Okay." He took a breath. He sat up and pulled his shirt down. He crossed his arms over his chest. "You've got my complete attention."

Stephanie felt her stomach lurch and wondered if she was going to be sick again. She swallowed hard and willed herself to hold on.

"This is hard to say. I didn't know until just a few days ago and I needed to tell you in person…."

"Yes?" he asked curiously. "What is it, Stephanie? What's wrong?"

"I'm expecting a baby. Your baby."

"A baby? You're pregnant…really?" His mouth hung open in surprise. She could see him trying to process the information and returning again to that shocked look. "You're sure?"

She nodded. "I'm positive. I did about ten of those home tests…and I'm even craving rice pudding."

He looked puzzled and frowned at her. "Rice pudding?"

"It's a long story…I'll explain later. The thing is, it was an accident. I just want you to know I wasn't out to trap you, or trick you… I hope you believe me," she said in a quieter voice.

"You're not the type to do something like that, Stephanie. I know that."

She still couldn't tell if the news had made him happy, but at least he didn't think she'd set out to trap him.

"I don't expect anything…honestly. I take full responsibility."

He smiled, looking very amused. "Very noble of you. But I think I had something to do with the situation."

"You know what I mean," she insisted.

He sighed and smiled at her. Then his expression turned serious again. "I think we should get married."

"Married?" Stephanie jumped up from her seat. It was the last thing she'd expected him to say. "You don't have to say that, Matt. Honestly."

He looked surprised at her reaction. "You don't sound very happy at the idea."

She glanced at him. "I'm sorry…you just surprised me. I don't want you to think you have to marry me, Matt. I wouldn't have ever even told you if I thought you were going to do this."

"Do what?" He stood up, too, looking upset, she thought. "Take responsibility for bringing a child into the world? I grew up without a mother for most of my childhood, Stephanie. I know what it's like to be in a one-parent family. I don't want my own son or daughter to go through that."

"But you told me you don't even want children," she reminded him.

"I felt that way when I was younger, that's true. But I feel differently now. This would be a perfect solution. I just never met a woman I wanted to start a family with. Until you, I mean," he added hastily.

She wasn't sure if he really meant that. Or was tacking it on to bolster his case. She felt so confused. This conversation wasn't going at all as she'd imagined.

"Besides, what will your family say? You're a nice girl from a nice family. I knew that from the minute I met you. You're not the type to do the unconventional thing. Your family won't let you," he pointed out to her.

"If I wanted to get married just to satisfy *them* I'd be Mrs. Tommy Torrelli by now," she reminded him tartly. "I'm not worried about what they think."

"Well, I am," he said with a short laugh. "I want them to know I want to do the right thing. The honorable thing. Especially your father."

When she didn't seem swayed, he drew closer, his voice growing softer and warmer. "Stephanie…we get along so well. We respect each other, we enjoy each other's company. We laugh together. We make glorious love…. You're the most wonderful woman I've ever met. I know you'll make a wonderful mother and a great wife. Why wouldn't this work?" he asked sincerely. "Just give me one good reason."

She gazed at his too-handsome, much beloved face and released a long sigh. She had a reason, a very good one, she thought. He'd never once in all this time said he loved her.

She didn't want him to marry her just to do the right thing, or because he thought they were "compatible." Or because he wanted to placate her family. She'd never feel happy or secure under those circumstances. She'd always be waiting for him to meet someone else. Someone new. Someone he could truly love. He owned her heart. But she didn't have his. It was that simple.

"It just wouldn't work. Believe me," she said finally. She looked at him, surprised to see a sudden, pained look in his expression.

He turned around and walked away from her. "All right. If you say so. You seem to have a very clear idea of what you want...and don't want." When he turned around, his expression was hard, unreadable. "I'm not going to beg you."

"I never wanted you to," she replied quietly.

"So...I guess I'll call my lawyer tomorrow. Draw up some sort of agreement for you to look at."

"Agreement?" He had lost her. What did his lawyer have to do with this. "About what?"

"Child support. Visitation...I will be allowed to see our baby, won't I? Or do you think that just won't work out either?"

She felt shocked by his cold, distant tone. "No...I mean, yes. Of course you can see our child. You'll be their father."

He nodded. "Well, thanks. At least you're willing to grant me that much."

He grabbed his jacket off the floor and headed for the door, brushing by her. "I hope you're seeing a good doctor?" He paused, his hand on the door knob.

"I have an appointment. Next week. My sister recommended the doctor. She says he's very good."

"All right. I just wanted to know. That's all."

She felt a sudden, almost overwhelming urge to run to him and hold him, thinking somehow that would set everything back to rights between them.

But it wouldn't solve anything, she knew. Nothing would ever be the same again.

Before she could say or do anything, he opened the door and walked out. "Good night, Stephanie," he said. "Goodbye."

Then he shut the door quickly, without waiting for her answer.

Angie and Jimmy returned from their honeymoon in Puerto Rico and rushed over to see Dominic straight from the airport. Fresh sympathetic faces took the heat off Stephanie, and she was able to avoid her family for the rest of the weekend. She hid away in her apartment, mulling over her problem and her possible solutions.

On Monday morning she returned to the hotel and her former job in the operations department. Her two-week vacation was over and she had to go back, though early that morning, between bouts of morning sickness and fears of facing Matt again, she seriously considered quitting altogether, right over the phone.

But she couldn't do that. For one thing it would look dreadful to any possible new employers. She had to think ahead, to her new responsibilities—supporting her baby. Though Matt had offered to help her—in a cold, legal way—she didn't count on that. He'd been infuriated with her finally, as upset as she'd ever seen him, and she wondered if he'd ever follow through on those promises.

Dressed in a gray suit and pale-blue blouse, she whirled her hair up and dabbed on a bit of makeup. Checking the time just before she left the apartment, she found the diamond-and-sapphire bracelet on her wrist and stared at it a moment, then took it off and put it away in her jewelry box. She'd have to return the bracelet to Matt. She couldn't keep it now. It would always remind her of their time together and she didn't need that weighing her down. A heart shattered in so many pieces was enough baggage, she decided.

Stephanie slipped into the hotel, wary of meeting up with Matt. Her fears were irrational to some degree, she knew. It was a huge hotel and he was constantly on the go. Before becoming his assistant, she'd hardly ever seen him. It wouldn't take much to avoid him while working here. Especially since she didn't plan on working here that much longer.

Over the weekend she'd figured out a plan and once she was back in her old office, she put the wheels in motion. She had a good friend from college who was the marketing director at a small hotel in San Francisco. Her friend had often tried to coax Stephanie out to the West Coast. Stephanie knew this was the time to take her friend up on the offer. Since Jillian knew her so well, she probably wouldn't even bother contacting Matt for a recommendation. If anyone would understand her circumstances and give her a break, it would be Jillian.

At midday, Stephanie called California and reached her friend right away. It was easy to announce that she was ready to transfer to the West Coast. Jillian was thrilled and even had a job opening she thought suited Stephanie perfectly. But Stephanie thought it best to lay all her cards on the table from the start and it was harder to explain that she was pregnant and trying to move out of town to get away from the child's father.

"I get it. You don't have to say more." Her friend

sighed and continued in a reassuring tone. "We're good friends, and I want to help you now any way I can."

Stephanie quietly thanked her, though it was hard to talk around the giant lump in her throat. It had always been hard for her to ask for help. Maybe because she was the oldest child of so many siblings and thought she was the one who always had to do the helping. Or maybe it was just her independent, self-sufficient nature. It was good to see that when she did turn to a friend, help was there for her. She so needed it right now.

"What about your family? What do they say about you moving so far away?"

"They don't know yet. The idea just came to me over the weekend. I guess I don't want to tell them until it's all settled."

"I see. And your baby's father, I guess he doesn't know either?" her friend asked.

"No, I can't tell him. He wants to outline visiting rights with a lawyer and all that sort of stuff. I'm afraid he'll find some legal way of making me stay in New York if I tell him."

"He sounds like a really great guy," Jillian said drily.

"He is," Stephanie insisted. "I mean, he's a good person. He's just upset right now because…I don't want to marry him."

It was hard to say the words out loud, she realized. Part of her did want to marry Matt. Wanted it with all her heart. But another part, the stubborn Rossi side, just wouldn't compromise, clinging to standards that had not been met.

Jillian didn't say anything right away. "Well, sounds

like you've got a lot going on. I can't wait to see you, Steph, and talk more in person."

They arranged for Stephanie to fly out to California at the end of the week for an official interview. She would leave Friday night and spend the weekend in California. She decided to tell her parents she was going on a business trip, which wasn't entirely a lie. She wasn't going to tell Matt anything and hoped they didn't meet up before then.

She quickly turned to her computer and booked her flight reservation, then printed out the confirmation. It seemed like a ticket to her freedom and she felt greatly relieved that so far, her plan was working out so well.

She was doing the right thing, Stephanie told herself. Matt would be angry at first when he learned she was taking the baby so far away, but he really didn't have any way to stop her. She couldn't stay in New York and see him all the time…and see him with the baby. It would just be too painful. If she moved away, he might come out a few times a year, but it would be much easier to handle.

Her family would be unhappy too, but Matt had been right about one thing. If they ever found out that he'd wanted to marry her, they'd drive her crazy about it. She had to get far away from all of them, both Matt and her family.

Stephanie worked hard for the rest of the afternoon, reconnecting with her co-workers and her old duties. It all seemed so dull and routine compared to being Matt's assistant. Another reason to leave, she realized. Although she'd felt as if she'd been to another solar system, everyone else accepted her return easily, as if she'd just been out with a cold for a few days. It was funny, she thought, how adaptable people are. They are not as conscious of you nearly as much as you think they are. All her life, she'd been too worried about making a good impression, about what other people thought. Well, now she was going to strike out on her own and flaunt her choices in the face of convention. Despite everything, that part felt good.

Late in the day, she was returning to her office with a cup of tea and some crackers to soothe her queasy stomach, when she found Nana sitting in an armchair, waiting for her.

"Oh, there you are. They said you should be right back."

"Hi, Nana." Stephanie leaned over and kissed her grandmother's cheek. "I didn't expect to see you here. I thought your job ended on Friday."

"It did. But I had to clean out my locker and return my uniform." Nana sighed and smiled. "I love that uniform. It made me feel so...official. But, I think I found myself a good job back in Carroll Gardens. I get to wear a uniform there, too."

"Really? Already? Gee, you don't waste any time, do you?"

Stephanie replied with a grin.

"At my age, dear, that's not an option."

"Where are you working?"

"At the triplex on Court Street. I'm going to work the snack bar on Super Senior Tuesdays."

"Wow, good job. You get to see all the movies for free, too, right?"

"That's right. It's a great perk. Not as exciting as working here. But the commute is easy. Rose can't wait.

She wants me to sneak her in for free...but I can't do that."

"Of course not," Stephanie replied.

Nana rearranged her tote bag, which rested across her lap. "So...did you tell Matt yet about the...you know what?"

Stephanie felt her cheeks grow warm. "Yes...I did. We had a...talk about it."

"A talk? Well, that sounds very modern." Nana's pale eyebrows jumped a notch. "So?"

"It's just not working out," she said honestly. "I told you this wasn't as simple as you thought it would be."

Nana gave her a serious look. "I see. Well...I just wanted to know if I should be expecting another wedding this summer. I'll postpone my trip to Alaska with Rose. She'll be ready to spit though, so you'd need to invite her."

Stephanie sighed. Dear Nana. She still didn't get it. There wasn't going to be any marriage to Matt. Not this summer, not ever.

"You go ahead with your plans, Nana. I don't think anything will change between me and Matt."

Nana sighed. She got up and walked around to Stephanie's side of the desk, then leaned over and gave her granddaughter a long hug. "You have to keep the faith, *bella*. Faith in love. Sometimes love is like a star hidden behind the clouds. Just because you don't see it, doesn't mean it's not there."

Stephanie swallowed hard. Her grandmother's perspective was sweet and romantic, but didn't renew her hope. Sometimes the star just wasn't there, she wanted to say. Sometimes it was all clouds.

The rest of the week was an uphill climb. Her trip to

California loomed in the distance, a light at the end of the tunnel and the only thing that kept Stephanie going. She saw the doctor on Wednesday for her first checkup and the baby became even more real. The doctor, a man in his late fifties, was serious and kind, asking few questions about the baby's father once Stephanie made it clear that he wouldn't be involved. But even avoiding the topic of Matt, she felt his absence even more keenly. He should have been with her, talking to the doctor, sharing the experience.

She hadn't heard a word from Matt, though on Wednesday night she'd found a thick manila envelope in her mailbox, marked Personal & Private with Matt's return address in the upper left-hand corner. The agreement from Matt's lawyers concerning the baby. Stephanie tossed it on her desk without even bothering to open it.

She'd begun to worry that Matt might try to keep her from moving away, though she didn't know exactly how he could do it. But he did have lots of money to spend on a legal battle and she'd heard of such custody suits before.

He wouldn't do that to her, would he? Just for revenge? She didn't think he'd be so cruel…but he had a dark side and she had to be realistic.

The fatigue of early pregnancy and getting back into the mix at her job gave Stephanie very little time or energy to worry about anything for too long. She'd come home at six and fall asleep in a heap on her bed. She'd get up again briefly at eight, force herself to eat a bowl of soup or some eggs and toast, then soon after, go back to sleep again until the morning.

On Thursday night, however, she had to forego the nap and pack her bag for California. She was going to leave for the airport very early the next morning and had to have everything in order. She showered quickly to wake herself up and dressed in her nightgown and robe, planning on an early bedtime.

She was midway through the process when it felt as if she just couldn't keep her eyes open. She dumped her open bag onto the bedroom floor, shut the light and dropped on the bed.

The sound of her front-door buzzer ringing woke her from a deep sleep. She lifted her head and pushed a wad of hair from her eyes, feeling totally disoriented. The bedside clock said 9:15 and she had no idea who could be visiting.

She hadn't even heard the buzzer ring, she realized as she hurried across the living room. But sometimes a guest came in the building along with a resident, or a delivery man.

"Who's there?" she called out before undoing the row of locks.

"It's me, Matt." When she didn't answer, he added. "Open up. I need to see you."

She sighed and tightened the belt on her robe. What was he doing here? It had to be about the papers from the law firm. She was probably supposed to answer in some way by now and he was annoyed about it.

Her mind raced for some excuse that would persuade him to leave, but she couldn't come up with anything that convincing.

"Stephanie…are you going to open this door? Or do I need to use the key?"

"The key? How did you get a key?"

"I have my sources," he replied calmly. Even through the thick door she could sense his smug smile.

Nana Bella! She'd never given her set of keys back. It had to be her…the little white-haired—correction, lately blond—traitor!

Knowing she was beat, she took a breath and pulled open the door. She looked a wreck, a complete bed head…but there was no help for it now.

"In that case, you might as well come in," she greeted him tartly, flinging open the door.

"Thank you," he said politely. He walked in, gazing around, as if he was a detective, scoping out a crime scene.

Stephanie faced him, her hands crossed tightly over her chest. "Looks like I woke you. I'm sorry," he said. " I didn't think you'd be asleep this early."

"Pregnant women conk out a lot, in case you didn't know."

He pursed his lips. "Sorry you're not feeling well…. Or maybe you just need to get up very early tomorrow? To catch an early flight to California for a job interview?"

She stared at him. "Don't be ridiculous. I'm not going anywhere. Who told you that?"

"A little bird told me. A little old bird from Brooklyn who keeps flying the coop."

Nana again? But how did she know? Stephanie thought back to the last time she'd seen her grandmother, when Nana had visited her office on Monday afternoon. The printout of her e-ticket and an e-mail confirming the interview had been on her desk, she realized, out in the open for anyone to see. Anyone who was nosy enough to go looking.

"That nosy little buttinsky!"

"She really takes the cake, doesn't she?" Matt agreed with a short laugh.

"What else did she tell you?" Stephanie asked angrily.

He shrugged. "Only that you're unbelievably stubborn...like your father, she claims. Nothing I didn't already know."

"This isn't funny!" she railed at him. "She had no right to tell you my private business and send you over here like this."

"Of course she did. She loves you very much and she wants you to be happy."

Stephanie heaved a long sigh. She knew that was true, but she didn't see how another confrontation with Matt would solve anything.

"I can't go through this again, Matt. We've said what we had to say. You're wasting your time here."

He frowned at her, his expression growing serious again. "Did you ever open that package I sent you?"

"No, I didn't get around to it. Is that what this is all about? Do you have some legal letter in there telling me I can't leave New York City without your permission?"

He sighed. "Not quite...I did put a letter in though." His gaze darkened as he stared at her. "I guess you didn't read it."

She felt her mouth grow dry. "No...I didn't...what did it say?"

"It said I was sorry for the way we fought the other night. The way I asked you to marry me...it just didn't come out right. I've had some time to think, Stephanie. It's hard for me, but I just have to tell you that I love you. I never thought I could ever feel this way about anybody and I have to admit, it scares the hell out of me. Maybe that's why I could never tell you sooner."

She gasped, feeling as if someone had just socked her squarely in the stomach. "You love me?"

He nodded slowly. "With all my heart. That's why I

want to marry you. The baby is just a magnificent bonus. I want to marry you and have a life with you. I want us to grow old together and have a big family and fuss and argue, just like your parents do…."

She shook her head wildly at him. "Please…*not* like my parents."

He laughed, a warm loving sound. Stepping closer, he reached out and rested his hands on her shoulders, forcing her to face him squarely.

"Like us then. Like two people who can't live without each other. I know I can't live without you. I love you so much, it's making me crazy."

"It's making me crazy, too," she admitted. "It already has." She jumped into his arms and held him as if she'd never let go. "I love you so much, Matt. More than I can ever say—"

Matt had definitely heard enough. He dipped his head, capturing her mouth in a deep soulful kiss. Stephanie felt as if she was floating out among the stars. It felt like a dream…but it was all too real to be denied.

What Nana had said was true. She'd been struck by lightning and Matt had too, and there was just no fighting it.

Hours later, after they had made love and fallen asleep in each other's arms, Stephanie woke to see Matt's smiling face beside her on the pillow.

She sighed and lifted her head on one elbow to see him better. "What about my family…tell the truth now. Are you sure they won't drive you crazy?"

"They might, after awhile. But I thought I'd buy your folks a condo in Florida. That should give us a break for a few months a year. We can't keep them away from their grandchildren. That wouldn't be right at all."

She grinned. "You've been thinking a lot about this, haven't you?"

"Night and day." He nodded, folding his arms behind his head. He was so gorgeous and sexy...she could hardly believe it. What did she do to deserve such a wonderful man? Stephanie wasn't really sure, but didn't want to question her good luck.

"Should we have our wedding at Casa Amalfi?" he asked her with a teasing grin. "I wouldn't want to break your father's record. If you have a reception there, cousin Vito is going to put up a plaque with your father's name on it. Just like the Baseball Hall of Fame."

"Let's just buy him a plaque," Stephanie suggested. "I was thinking of something a bit more...sedate."

"I'm seeing a sculpture of the Brooklyn Bridge...in paté."

"Better make it actual size, out of pepperoni. My mother's going to invite the entire borough."

"Let her," he laughed. He pulled her close, ready to make love all over again. "We have a lot to celebrate."

Stephanie couldn't agree more. She'd be celebrating every day, thankful to some lucky star for bringing this wonderful man, this wonderful love, into her life.

* * * * *

Silhouette®

SPECIAL EDITION™

PRESENTING A NEW MINISERIES BY

RaeANNE THAYNE:

The Cowboys of Cold Creek

BEGINNING WITH

LIGHT THE STARS

April 2006

Widowed rancher Wade Dalton relied
on his mother's help to raise three small
children—until she eloped with "life coach"
Caroline Montgomery's grifter father! Feeling
guilty, Caroline put her Light the Stars
coaching business on hold to help the angry
cowboy...and soon lit a fire in his heart.

DON'T MISS THESE ADDITIONAL BOOKS IN THE SERIES:

DANCING IN THE MOONLIGHT, May 2006
DALTON'S UNDOING, June 2006